What most readers don't understand is that authors thrive best where people leave deserving reviews or pass on the feeling that remains with them after they finish the book. Beside telling all your friends about it, please, if you can spare the time, leave a review of **A Day for Tigers** wherever you purchased it from.

Thank you

Cybermouse Books

Copyrights;

Cybermouse MultiMedia Ltd.,
101 Cross Lane
Sheffield S10 1WN

www.cybermouse-multimedia.com

First published by Cybermouse Books 2015

In the design of this book, Cybermouse Multimedia Ltd. have
made every effort to avoid infringement of any established copyright.
If anyone has valid concern re any unintended infringement please contact
us first at the above address.

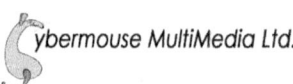

A Day for Tigers

A Collection of the

Weird and Wonderful

from the imagination of

Bill Allerton

This book contains themes that seem to recur in my work, old favourites such as Trains, Mice, Sex, Pain, Salt, Music, Tigers and Surgery. Odd elements, you might suggest. I might suggest that you are right, too. But all of these things are not subjects in themselves, they are pivots that we, as humans, pinwheel around giving off sparks. So this is not a collection of stories, it's a collection of sparks, given off by the friction of the dilemmas that my protagonists find themselves in.

If these sparks don't jump in the way that you would expect them to, then look around you. Do you understand everything and everyone you see?

In here is sarcasm, darkness and fear, dry humour, and a need for the suspension of your disbelief. But there is also hope and a lack of political correctness (the impending doom of the modern world) plus sexuality in all its desires and different forms.

If you are looking for a single thread to follow through this collection then you are looking in vain. If you wish to be surprised (and I hope delighted) by the change of direction presented in each story, then this is the book for you.

My dearest wish is that you open your mind to any eventuality, sit back, and travel with me along unfamiliar tracks of discovery...

Bill Allerton

Contents:

Appendix: Other Titles in the Cybermouse Books range

The author would like to take this opportunity to thank;

Ray Bradbury, Isaac Asimov, Arthur C. Clarke, Alfred Bester, Larry Niven, Clifford D. Simak, A. E. Van Vogt, John Wyndham, Philip K. Dick, Lester Del Rey, Poul Anderson, James Blish, Robert A. Heinlein, Frederik Pohl, Fritz Leiber, Jack Vance, Robert Silverberg, John W. Campbell Jnr., Jack Williamson, Harry Harrison, Theodore Sturgeon, C. M. Kornbluth and Robert Sheckley...

just for having existed...

This book is dedicated to

William James and Edward Lewis
Allerton

Who arrived Bright & Beautiful
On the morning of
26th. November 2015

The V8 Morning

In a spirit of attempting to demonstrate where inspiration has it's roots, I'd like to tell you where the spark for this story came from.

I live in a row of stone-built terraces and, when I'm sat in our small conservatory, I can look out across our postage-stamp-sized garden to a row of outbuildings. The roofs to these are covered in Virginia creeper and are wonderful to behold as it turns crimson in autumn.

The roofs are capped with flat, wide, Yorkstone topping stones which catch the summer sun from late morning until early evening. I began to notice that a succession of cats would bask along the top of these warm stones and I, for one, could only envy them.

One day, for a brief spell, there were two cats on there. Cats are usually solitary creatures but these two faced each other for a while, then sat down a distance apart, glancing at each other occasionally as if waiting for the other one to make a move.

I do remember that one was a warm-looking ginger cat. I honestly can't remember the other one now but I began to wonder what they were saying to each other, or would have been saying if they were not cats, and just ordinarily weird like you and I.

The V8 Morning

Watching from the corner of his eye, Arthur marvelled at her rigidity, tucking far back into his memory the purse of her lips, the sight of her mouth set in grim determination of purl one, plain two, and the way the crows feet around her eyes fell as stress lines through age-metalled skin.

She looked no different than she had for as long as he'd known her. Maybe even a little younger, for there was an air of anticipation in the slender lines of her mouth today... and the blue eyes above it were just so. The skin of her nose, burned dark and flaking as they all were since the ozone burn-off, showed pink beneath.

And in the way her motor was always running.

He smiled as he rocked gently on the sunshine shelf.

'You're looking at me again,' she said.

Arthur would have sworn her eyes never so much as flickered.

'So?'

'So? So like I was an old truck... or something.'

'Haven't thought about one of those for a long time,' said Arthur.

'You're a liar,' said Marie.

Arthur locked his fingers together, cracked them quietly in the dark air and looked away. Marie pulled another yard off the ball into the silence. The bright clatter of the needles began again.

'So why do you think I came here today?'

'To listen,' said Arthur, '...to an old man's lies, by the sound of it.'

By the time she had reached the sunshine shelf that morning, Arthur was already there. He had reached down through the frost haze to help her over the last few crumbling blocks.

'Thought you weren't going to make it.'

Marie took a deep breath and hitched herself up onto the tumbled stone.

'You know I wouldn't miss today.'

He'd let go of her hand as soon as she was settled.

'Well, I know how it is.'

'No, you don't,' Marie had snapped.

She pulled up the dark leather bag beside her and popped the stud.

'I don't tittle-tattle about my family.'

'Yes, you do,' said Arthur.

Marie reached inside the bag and pulled out a ball of pale, crinkly wool and two slender needles. Arthur narrowed his eyes at her.

'Only what's not important...' she said.

In the pale light she tied on the wool and spun it deftly around two fingers. The needles began to flash in her hands, a solitary insect chitter in the tree-less dawn.

'Then how was it?' said Arthur.

Marie pulled a yard free from the ball in her lap.

'You know how it is,' she said.

In the space of a drawn breath, the horizon lit quietly with a thin strand of yellowish green. Arthur leaned forward to peer as if the act of leaning would bring it within reach of his failing sight. Marie changed direction and the loops slid swiftly from the left needle onto the right.

'You're a wonderful old bugger,' she said, 'You know that?'

Arthur tipped back his head to the stone behind him, opening his eyes to the last star.

'I wish you wouldn't do that,' he said.

The tiredness in his voice told Marie that he'd been awake most of the night, letting the darkness carry him into morning on its silent, remorseless carriage.

'Do what?'

Arthur waited until the black around the star had faded to palest blue. For a moment it seemed to brighten then, as if a mist took it, it was gone.

'You know,' he said.

'I do know,' said Marie, 'But it's one of those things I do because...' she rounded on him then, needles bristling the air between them, '...because sometimes you shut yourself away in that old head. And because using plain words with you is like... like taking a stick to a tortoise.'

And it was also something to do with the way she felt about him, although she would never tell him that. And it gave him such a jolt every time she swore. But mostly it was just... fun. She allowed herself a glimpse of the dawn, then cast on again.

'You're a wonderful old bugger,' she said.

'And you're the most provocational, irrationable excuse for a woman I ever met.'

Arthur shrugged his coat around his shoulders, fastening the top button.

'And for once can you stop that interminable knitting?'

Marie smiled to herself.

'No,' she said.

Arthur took the ball of wool from her lap and threw it down the stone pile. Marie watched as the wool bounced cleanly from each one, unravelling and billowing pale in the thin morning air.

'I take back the 'wonderful',' she said, 'What did you do that for?'

'I don't need it today,' said Arthur, 'The needles I mean. Clicking and clacking away like there were still insects in the world. Making me remember things, like...'

'Like old trucks?' said Marie.

'Yes...' snapped Arthur, '...like old trucks.'

Marie pursed her mouth. This time the crows feet skewed, bending under the thrust of a dark humour within. She pulled back a yard of wool from the clinging stone and the needles resumed their bright-winged chitter.

'How many times have you knitted that wool?' said Arthur, 'Bet you can't tell me that.'

'Seven,' said Marie, 'First it was a cardigan. Fact'ry made.'

She rummaged in the depths of her bag.

'Still have the label somewhere... never mind.'

She sat up straight and pushed the bag along the broken stone wall.

'Found it in a basement, up against the Castle wall. Dark blue. Pearl buttons. Then it was a jumper for Stephen but he soon grew out of it. Let's see...'

She paused a moment, thinking into the silence as if holding back the dawn in her breath. She let it go in a rush.

'Leggings for Jamie. Bodice for Laura. Pullover for Stephen. Without the sleeves there was enough wool for the body. Don't know how she's grown him that big on what we have to eat. Then it was a shawl for me...'

'Enough,' said Arthur, 'But why knit today? Shouldn't today be different?'

Marie breathed in something of the surrounding darkness, somehow lightening the mood between them. At that moment, the sun seeped pale over the horizon, pushing the black shades and depths of blue behind the broken shoulders of cut stone and fallen buttresses into the land of once-was.

She exhaled, her breath curling the cool air with its silver mist.

'Different?'

The needles fell silent in her hands and she rested them in her lap for a moment.

'If we were to do something different,' she said, 'It'd mean that what we've had these last years was just a sort of waiting game. Waiting for the old ways to come back.'

She shuddered and pulled at the wool again, 'As if once wasn't enough. Don't you see that?'

The needles resumed their chafing as she quickly looped the yarn around the end. She poked one stitch and stopped again.

Arthur sat silent, feeling defeated and lost against the cool expanse of sandstone beneath his withered old thighs. He reached down and pulled the yarn back for her.

'But there are things I wish for...' he said.

'Like an old truck,' said Marie.

Arthur nodded slowly in the deep, desert chill, searching through the bright, stilled needles in his head and finding only frustration amongst worn-out old reasons and past ridicule.

'I don't see why I should feel any shame in that,' he said at last.

'And why should you?' said Marie.

'Well, you just said…'

'Ways,' said Marie, 'I was talking about ways. Old trucks is a thing.'

'But you said…'

Arthur took the look of her face and retreated.

'I never did understand your pre-occupation with the damn things anyway,' said Marie.

Arthur placed his hands beside him on the cold stone. Gripping the edge, he rocked silently back and forth feeling the compacted sand tug hard against his skin.

He stopped, his eyes fast to the east where the bow of golden light crested the horizon. The growing light patch-worked the land with midnight hollows, appearing and disappearing as randomly as the holes in the long road of his memory.

The sun's arc picked out the expanse of broken stone around them in its glow. Dust motes lifted silently from the collapsed profusion of pinnacles, solid oak rafters, needles and purlins. Shadows haunted the faces of dry-mouthed, shattered gargoyles.

For what might have been the thousandth time, Arthur held out his hands and began to explain.

'You see…' he said. The sun flickered through his fingers, staining them gold and black. '…this is where a truck begins.'

Smiling in quiet self-satisfaction, Marie pulled back another yard. The rising click of the needles served only to bait the tortoise further.

'It could have sat out there in the street all day,' said Arthur.

He studied his fingers minutely, creased the swollen joints, one by one.

'…but without these it was nothing. Takes a man to work a truck.'

'What time is it?' asked Marie.

'It's scheduled for twelve.'

'No,' she said, scolding him gently, 'What time is it now?'

'Hold on,' said Arthur. He looked around for the metal bar they'd pried loose so long ago the day was now lost in the emptied garage of his mind. He slotted it into the hole worn patiently in the stone beside them and studied the dial scratched into the surface.

'Make it… 'bout six o'clock.'

Marie looked down to the foot of the mound and assessed the size of the ball of yarn. She slipped the needles into one hand while the fingers of the other pried loose the top three buttons of her jacket, leaving the rest secure against a sudden dust from a quick, early breeze.

'Trucks,' she said.

'As I was saying,' said Arthur. He held up his hands once more, 'Without these…'

Marie closed her eyes. This would keep him going for around two hours. The needles clicked gently to the remembrance of her fingers.

Three or four days ago, on a morning just like this one was set to be, Jamie and Stephen had glistened like nuggets in the sun. Sweat-lacquered and young inside their golden skin they'd loaded the last things onto the cart. Marie had watched them flex without creasing, bend without feeling the tendency to break. Perhaps things would be different after all… but not until tomorrow.

Laura had hugged arms around her from behind.

'Mom. This is the last chance. We can't wait any longer.'

'Then you'd better get going.'

Looking up, Marie shaded her eyes to see the dust plume wavering the western horizon. It had been there all afternoon.

'There are others over there. If you get off now you'll catch their tail. They'll know where it's safe. We had cousins in Southwell. Try there. But don't use my married name. Someone might remember.'

'But, Mom.'

'Go,' said Marie. She hugged each one in turn and then they left; the children silent, their faces damp and drying in the heat of the day.

Marie had watched them for a few minutes until she was sure they could no longer see the lines of her face, the fold of her eyes, the crumple of her mouth, then went inside.

The needles busied and chittered for an age until they fell quite still.

'Sleeping jacket for Laura.'

Arthur jerked back from a horizon where the sun was high, the road ran straight for ever and the tarmac was hot and singing with tyres in the morning heat.

'What? Oh… I see.'

The gearbox of his mind shifted slowly down. He began to crawl along beside her. Mentally pacing. Like slow traffic.

'That's six,' said Marie.

'How was it when they left?' said Arthur, 'You didn't ever say.'

Marie pulled another yard back. The loose end trailed up the first step and curled itself around like a cat's tail in the sunlight.

'Ever thought there might be a reason for that?'

'Yes,' said Arthur, 'but it never stopped you before and if today's not about 'different', then I think I've every reason to expect an answer. Sometime.'

He studied the metal bar where it poked from its dial in the flat stone.

'Sometime soon.'

'Oh, you know how it is,' said Marie.

'Yes,' said Arthur. 'I think I do.'

'No, you don't,' said Marie, 'You're just guessing. Like always.'

Arthur screwed up his eyes to watch the sun climb the inevitable blue wall of sky.

'They tried a lot of things,' he said, 'Reminded you of things you never knew you'd forgotten, just to convince you to go with them.'

He closed his eyes and drifted back against the carved stone.

'They waxed your importance to their life like it was a new car.'

The needles fell silent as Marie stopped to listen.

'They took the lines from your face and reminded you of how you'd earned each and every one,' Arthur said, 'Polished them out, they did, one at a time. When that didn't work they took a handful of leather and buffed your pride until you didn't know you were made of such reflection.'

He smiled behind closed eyes, watching with the sun in his face, listening to the air with his tongue, tasting the growing heat in the sharp, stone smell of the desert.

'Until you shone like a great and priceless carriage.'

He opened his eyes then and turned towards her, blinking in the new light.

'And what did you do?'

The needles picked up their beat in the growing sun. Marie held her face straight as a poker, hitched up another yard and watched the end uncoil lazily to climb another step.

'I told them,' she said, 'that at my age I was only fit to be a hearse.'

Closing her eyes, a laugh, silent and honest, caught her throat. It took hold of Arthur like a spark and they sat slowly rocking on the sunshine shelf until there was nothing left of the sound but the tears streaming down their faces.

In the small introspective quiet that followed, Marie's hand reached across the stone between them and touched upon his.

'I was married here,' she said, 'In a small chapel off the south transept.'

'I know that,' said Arthur.

'Shush,' said Marie, 'I was reminding myself.'

Arthur undid the last button on his ragged jacket. He stared out, watching the dust flick and spin amongst the ruins of the lower city, feeling it's silk in every fold of his skin.

'I never went to Horncastle but the once.'

'Too late now to go again,' said Marie.

'So it makes it all the more improbable…' said Arthur, still watching the desert as if something of interest might take place amongst the sand, '…that there's a man out there.'

Marie hitched up another yard.

'What's he thinking,' said Arthur, 'I mean… right now. What is he thinking?'

'Probably looking at that button right now,' said Marie.

The needles held silent and still for a moment as her mind's eye saw the unlocked button as a hammer, with a dull, square, metal head and slender shaft of whitened wood.

'Probably looking at it and wondering how heavy it's going to feel at that moment.'

'Wonder if he's picked it up?' said Arthur.

'Picked what up?'

'That hammer you're thinking about,' he said.

'How'd you know what I'm thinking about?'

Arthur smiled and held up his arms as if the hands gripped the steering wheel of a long-forgotten truck.

Marie shrugged her shoulders and tied off the row.

'Many times,' she said, 'He's picked it up and weighed it in his mind. Swung it a time or two, just to get the balance. Then he's looked at it again and put it down, not quite believing.'

'But what's he thinking?'

Arthur creased his brow, trying to project himself into the mind of a man out there alone and unprotected in the heat of the desert.

'How does he see it?'

The needles click slowed as she cast back onto the left.

'The end of an age,' said Marie, 'Probably feels responsible too.'

'For God's sake, Marie…'

She jumped at his unaccustomed use of her name.

'…he only drove a truck.'

'Makes him no less a part of it,' said Marie, 'In fact, quite fitting in a way.'

'He only feels responsible because you made him feel that way,' snapped Arthur, 'Leastways, people like you.'

'People like me?' said Marie. She hitched up another yard, 'Let's see… You mean people that spent thirty years hiding in holes. People that watched their children's children born with bits missing or god-placed on the wrong end and people that had to give up all the things that made life what they thought it was? For God's Sake yourself, Arthur. What wouldn't you give for another car… or an old truck?'

She rummaged in the bag beside her.

'Almost forgot. Brought you something.'

She placed a small bundle in his hand. The rag was damp with oil and had a small piece of familiar yarn tied around it. Arthur undid it carefully. Inside were two keys, bright with chrome. Attached to them was a black plastic fob with 'Ford' enamelled across it.'

"08 Galaxy',' said Marie, watching the growing intensity of his face.

'V8. 3 litre. Six speeds. 7 Seater.'

Arthur stared at her in amazement.

'Dark Blue Metallic Paint,' she said.

Arthur held the keys to his forehead, letting the metal seep into his skin and from there through to his brain, igniting his imagination.

'Hide Seats in Lemon,' said Marie.

'Don't tell me,' said Arthur, 'Let me feel it.'

Marie watched him from the corner of her eye.

'Electric Windows.'

'Stop it,' said Arthur, 'Stop it.'

'Power Roof.'

'No. Please,' he said, 'Just… let… me…'

She tucked the needles more firmly under her arms.

'Independent All-Round Suspension.'

'Please!' said Arthur.

'Four Wheel Drive.'

'No!'

'Traction Control. Limited Slip Differential.'

'I give up,' said Arthur, and handed back the keys.

'You see,' said Marie, 'It's no good is it? You've been hanging on to the wrong things. This is a day for letting go.'

'Just tell me one thing,' said Arthur, 'Was it really yours?'

'Bought it here in Lincoln,' she said.

She took up the keys in one brown hand and threw them as far as she could across the sand.

'Kept it right up to GZ Day. Came out from the hole weeks after and there was just so much twisted and burned metal it was impossible to tell if it was even there. And if it had been I couldn't ever have told you which part of it was mine. So I decided to forget it.'

She shrugged almost imperceptibly, but Arthur could see that it had marked a change in her thoughts.

'The keys…' he said, '…you kept them…'

Marie ignored him, a curious look taking her face as she sacrificed another button to the growing heat.

'How'd you afford it?' asked Arthur, 'Times were difficult, even before…'

'I had good work.'

Arthur's thoughts drifted away from the sharp edges of her reply and safely back to the man with the hammer.

'Hope he'll be alright,' he said.

He smiled inwardly, feeling his place in this now more than ever. And that was fitting too. On this, the day of the last bomb. The one it seemed no one left alive either wanted or knew how to take apart.

'Who?' said Marie. Her eyes followed his out across the sand.

'Oh, sure. He's the lucky one.'

She pulled up another yard and settled the needles.

'Ever been mad at them?' she asked.

'Mad at who?' replied Arthur. His eyes were focused upon a spot it was impossible for him to see, fifteen miles across the dry Lincolnshire desert.

'Jesus!' said Marie, 'Who else is there to be mad at in this whole left-over, bedraggled world? The people who made the bombs, of course.'

'But they're all dead,' said Arthur, 'Don't you think that's a waste of good emotion?'

Marie lowered the knitting to her lap and peered out over the sun-blasted wolds with their lace of emptied drains and dykes, remembering them flashed with ice over dark water, or green with algae and bright-quick-livid with fish.

'There's one left,' she said.

'He only a drove a truck,' replied Arthur.

Marie's eyes fell dark and hooded by the overhead sunlight.

'But all the same,' she said, '…for it to work, someone had to drive a truck.'

'I drove a truck,' said Arthur.

'Different kind of truck.'

'You don't know that,' said Arthur, turning to read the sundial beside him, 'It's eleven thirty… And I didn't always know what was in the truck.'

'You knew what it wasn't though, didn't you? You knew it wasn't bombs and such?'

'I suppose so.'

Arthur held the metal stick up straight, the heat from it burning his fingers and making them dance along its length.

'Maybe eleven forty…' he said, '…but it might have been parts. I wouldn't know if there were parts. They might have said they were… tractor parts …or something.'

'The trouble with parts,' said Marie, '…is you can learn how to put them back together again. That's why we have to make sure there's none left. But you didn't know. That's the difference.'

'For God's sake Marie, he's only an old truck driver. Let him go at last.'

'I suppose you're right,' said Marie, 'We all know what old truck drivers have for brains. Still, I envy him in a way. It's like ringing in the New Year. Remember that?'

Arthur stared into the mound of cast-down rubble around him, thinking of the time when the years hadn't all been just the same and all this old stone was stacked up vertically into the twin towers of God's House on top of Lincoln Hill, and sometimes it had been cold …and there had been bells enough for everyone to ring.

'I think,' said Marie, '…he should take all of that anger we couldn't learn to get shot of, and wind it into this old arm of his…'

She lifted her clenched fist high into the air.

'I bet it's strong,' said Arthur, 'I bet it's still full of sinew and muscle from lugging that old truck around.'

Lowering her fist, Marie bounced his arm lightly with it.

'He'll swing down that hammer for all of us…' she said, '…and ring in the Newest Year.'

The final yard of yarn crept over the top step as the needles broke the silence that followed her words.

Arthur opened his mouth to speak, then closed it again. There really was nothing much to say. Marie was right. Today was a day for holding on to what you'd come to believe in and wearing it like an overcoat packed ready and warming for the long winter. Not for wondering about other people… and keys… and keys… and suddenly the taste of fuel, hidden all these years where he least expected it, filled his mouth. He searched his brain for the quick cognitive spark he knew was there. The explosion that followed flooded his thoughts, depressing the piston of his tongue; cranking out the hollow-boned connecting rod of his arm to make one crooked finger point across the sand.

'Hey…' he said.

The keys spat harsh sunlight back at him and he laughed at their bright, useless fire, forty-years dead, that still dared to splash the dark crevices of the lower ranks of stone and light their shard crystals of stained glass. He sat back, laughter and surprise exhausted.

'All this time,' he said, 'All this time of torment and shame... and you're no different to me.'

He fiddled with the metal stick again. In the creak of steel wearing away at stone he found a reassurance in the thought that nothing lasts forever. He pulled it from the stone and threw it down amongst the rubble.

'It's almost time,' he said, 'Two or three minutes. No more.'

'Think it'll work?'

'It has to,' said Arthur.

They leaned back together against the cascade of arches, pillars and parapets behind them. Arthur squinted up at the sun, just by way of reminding himself who and where he was. Marie stared east across the vale-turned-desert to where she knew there was a man consumed in this moment by a righteous anger and fear. She could feel the weight of the hammer of her own heart. Knew that by her own hand she was as guilty as the man who drove the truck ...if only because all she had done was stand and watch others turning screws ...connecting wire traces to slickly-machined parts.

And all under her direction.

'Why didn't you go with them?' said Arthur.

'I want it to be different,' she said, 'I don't want us to go back around rotating history like it was some scuff mark on the rim of an old truck tyre. But 'different' won't happen unless I'm out of the way.'

Arthur nodded her attention towards the horizon, although nothing new had appeared.

'Too late to worry about that.'

He lifted his arm to run his fingers through the slender dark bars of his hair, sand sifting gently from the upturned cuff of his sleeve.

'Today's the day the wheel comes off.'

'Then before it does,' she said, 'You'd better remind me how it all went.'

Arthur cracked his swollen knuckles, one hand at a time. Out of habit, Marie stopped him. Her fingers deftly removed the last rows from the needles and she laid them carefully aside as if they were the last insect in the world …as if they were fragile things, like this man who sat beside her because he didn't know where else he could be today, and who couldn't ever forget the smell of petrol and oil, and perhaps at that last moment there just might be a whiff again of chemical, enough to keep him happy for all eternity.

Beyond the fallen stone and cruciform shadows, and the keys that lay twisted in the sun, a rose blossomed, white and pale.

'Close your eyes!' snapped Arthur.

Against her better instinct, Marie obeyed.

The ring of light passed through them and kept on going beyond the ruins and the caravans of people making their way still over the horizon.

'It's alright now,' said Arthur, 'That part has passed.'

They opened their eyes to see a mushroom cloud that stained the huge, tumultuously cathedral sky. Marie's fingers tied off the last of the yarn and stretched out the material, pulling it quickly into shape. A first touch of a final breeze glanced her cheek, bringing with it the faint scent of burning sand, somehow mixed with the tang of exploded petro-chemicals.

She turned to look at Arthur who was already tasting the air, drawing it into his lungs and savouring something of another age. She watched his face as his thoughts turned finally inward. A suspicious thought, struggling for the last hour to clear the thicket of his mind, surfaced into sharp clarity. Suddenly he peered at the keys, as if seeing them again for the first time.

'You...'

'Shush,' said Marie ...and the sound of her voice softened the furrowed frown on his face. Leaning over, her trembling fingers lovingly wrapped the scarf around his neck and tucked the ends into the open vee of his shirt.

'Here,' she said, 'There's going to be a wind today.'

Browsing

As Terry Pratchett once similarly said in an article, 'Everyone writes the 'Mystery Bookshop' short story when they are setting out.'

This bookshop usually has a hidden room with a book as the trigger to open a secret door and then whisk you away to the literary equivalent of Barsoom/Narnia/Discworld where you can Superhero/Spy/Magick your heart out.

These bookshops are all about new beginnings and the realisation of inner dreams of super-transcendence of all the ills of society, and your own distorted, unsatisfactory life in particular.

Jung or Freud may have liked to comment on that last statement, but they're not here right now. All you have is me. So stay with me, we're going somewhere... unlike Doug... who was only browsing, really...

Browsing

The books racked unevenly along the shelf as if each spine vied for Doug's attention. He picked a volume at random but his fingers slipped across the leather-grain cover as if they didn't wish to be a part of it. He tried to open it but couldn't hold it still long enough for it to let him inside to share the pages and the musty waiting-ness of a second-hand book.

Doug put it back before he dropped it.

He took a moment to look around. The shop was quiet on one of those days where rain can offer only puddles, and the sun a pale reflection along a pale street in February, the least distinct month of the year.

Doug hadn't noticed the shop before, although the district wasn't unfamiliar as a kind of passing-through place, and now that he was inside he found walls aged with bitter wallpaper greens and dark Victorian brown lacquers. On other days, winter browsers with their warm, knee-length overcoats might dispel the silence, their small dogs tied patiently to drainpipes outside the door and the shop echoing to the sound of their polite coughing.

Today though, it was just Doug, and the sound of someone rustling around like dried leaves behind the curtain over against the back wall.

He picked up another volume and that too slid through his fingers before coming to rest against the raised lapel of his jacket. Patiently he fumbled it back onto the shelf before lifting his fingers and stroking them against the pad of his thumb. He shrugged and reached for another book.

'May I help you?'

The voice jarred Doug's arm from its path and he turned around. A small dark man, with skin the colour of leaves in their autumn heaps of copper and gold, had appeared beside him. His voice was dry with the sound of birds nesting. The colours lapped his skin like pin feathers where the sparse silver grain of hair met his scalp. Outside, Doug realised, the wind might have pushed this man across a season into winter, a season to which he himself tried never to listen.

He stepped back and, with the sound of a thousand rushes dry on a dark night, the man followed him.

'May I help you?'

Doug's throat parched and the words clung to his tongue like moss on a rock.

The man smiled, lighting the shadow of his face with pearl.

'You were just browsing. I know. I saw the bus...'

He turned around to face the window.

In the pale daylight the mans clothes were creased and layered so they seemed to move and slide one over the other as he turned, the jacket fitting like a child's hand-wrapping in brown paper.

Doug half expected the trousers to be frayed at the cuff; birch twig besoms chafing, showering dusts of leaf as he moved. He took a step forward and something crushed and whispered beneath his feet.

He looked across the street to where the bus perched as if it had staggered to a halt on one front wheel and been unable to rise again. The control light on the road works flashed red then green, flickering patiently in the headlights of stalled cars.

'Buses,' said the man.

Doug swallowed and found his voice.

'Mostly reliable.'

The man nodded gently.

'Oh yes, …mostly.'

The man moved further along the window and Doug found himself following the sweet moss-scent of his skin.

Across the road a border of cones had been raised, splashing red and white into the puddle shimmer. Doug watched as two men in coveralls manoeuvred a large piston jack into place beneath the axle. One of them pumped the handle while men in dark uniforms moved ominously closer.

The man turned away from the window and smiled up at Doug.

'Timing, you see… is everything.'

As the man spoke there was autumn in his breath, where Doug himself breathed like the mid-summer rub of book on leather on wood. They stood for a moment, mingling seasons, with the books surrounding them perched high along the dark, fast-flowing rivers of mahogany shelf. As always, Doug was fascinated by the weight of papers, and their capacity to hold words pushed so heavily into them. As a reader, he'd found the sanctity of their language a responsibility sometimes too hard to bear.

He pulled himself away from that thought.

'They'll send a replacement,' he said.

He watched lines chafe across the man's face as he replied.

'They usually do.'

The man stroked his finger along a dark stream of shelf, rubbing patiently at the brass scroll corner plate.

Doug looked across the road, unsure of himself and the man, unsure of the sounds and smells that led his thoughts a season away, back into late fields with bright high moons and crushed silvered stalks.

He scanned the shop, trying to decide which of the numerous racks was hiding the door from his sight.

The mans voice tugged him gently back.

'You won't need it.'

Doug peered through the space above a double row of books, all slim and tightly bound with the same leather... and identically grained as the first he had touched. He was angry now.

'Which way did I come in?'

The man's face was cast in sudden shadow. Doug felt he ought to apologise. The sudden change in mood was alien to him, but the way the shop slid itself around him with its bitter-warm colour and leather-bound reassurance was deeply unsettling.

'I'm sorry. You were right... I was only browsing.'

The man smiled in return.

'There is only one way in.'

Doug paced the wall alongside the window and rubbed his hands over the embossed grapes and tart apple greens of the wallpaper where he had assumed the door to be. He would have sworn to it having been there; a small recess in the depth of the brickwork wearing dark years of varnish, and a bell hung silent on the end of its brass spring waiting for the catch plate to set it tingling in his memory like... like it never did.

'How did you know I was here?' said Doug, 'The bell never rang.'

'I knew someone would come to replace me,' said the man, 'Just the way I did.'

Doug stared over him to the window and looked outside. The bus was more upright now and the men in coveralls were standing silent while the uniforms were bent and attentive to something flowing like a dark river from beneath the radiator.

He placed both hands against the glass, just to feel them real, the cold etching into the joints.

The man moved up beside him and together they watched the scene across the road. In their reflection, Doug thought, they made a crude imbalance... with himself the full ripe here-and-now, skin pushed from beneath by a promise of Time to come... and the man beside him... a dry, flaking husk from which life had stolen every passage and fluid.

Across the road, the men untangled something vaguely human from beneath the axle, wrapped it in a shroud and carried it away. Doug couldn't see what it was but the man's reflection beside his smiled and nodded.

'Who are you?' said Doug.

The man reached a darkly-thumbed volume from a nearby shelf. He serried the leaves with a finger until it opened at a page.

With a pen brushed casually from his pocket, the man drew a line through Doug's name, then handed him the book and pen.

'I was The Book Keeper,' he said.

Mac's Elbow

I don't know if anyone recalls the sorely-missed website 'Urbis.com'. This was a unique place for writers of all stages of ability to meet and ask their peers for pointers or approval of ideas, styles, or indeed, long, completed works. They could also hope to be spotted by the agents who were invited to trawl the site for talent.

I spent some time on there amongst the poets and found incredible works in the least expected of places. It became a one-stop shop for inspiration for a time and I built up a collection of friends and acquaintances who disappeared abruptly along with the site one winters day.

So... lacking the inspiration from Urbis, I decided to put out a challenge on my website for ideas that I had to fulfil by writing them into a story or poem.

My friend 'Aeppel' in California challenged me to write a story about 'body parts' with the emphasis on 'elbow'.

It took a while to decide *whose* elbow would be the most important and life-changing body part, but once I formed the idea, this story wrote itself almost non-stop.

And in case you never heard of the Ford Edsel, it was a huge fiasco of 'futuristic' styling with it's enormously ugly radiator grille that resembled, by uncharitable comparison at the time, 'a vagina or a horsecollar'. A popular joke was that it resembled an Oldsmobile sucking a lemon.

Named after Edsel Ford, son of Henry, it was introduced to the American public on 'E' day, September 4th. 1957 and discontinued three years later. It has since become extremely collectable, and a tag of $100,000 (and rising) is not unusual today.

Mac's Elbow

From the way Mac felt as he sat on the edge of the treatment bench, being six feet below ground seemed more than appropriate. In the corner was the high level window that looked out through the shelter of the dugout to the rim of the 'Scheister Motors' stand. Between the rusted metal frame of the window and the decaying edge of the distant concrete, the evening star appeared. He watched its slow burn, letting it soak in through his retinas to obscure the pain.

Doc turned his elbow gently into a folded position.

'Let me tape that to your side.'

'No, Doc. I need the pain.'

'Nobody needs pain.'

'How else do I know I'm still alive?'

Doc shrugged his shoulder and began to pack his bag. Through the window Mac saw the concrete steps of the stand darken as Coach turned off the last of the floods.

'It's your funeral…'

'Never thought I'd be here to see it though, Doc.'

'Guess that's kind of unique... I guess...'

Doc folded his glasses and slid them into the pocket of his holdall.

'There has to be something else you can do... coaching perhaps?'

'Doc... if you couldn't do medicine... could you just stand around and watch? Would you have the patience to watch 'em fumble and stutter when you could... you know...?'

Doc heaved his bag from the leather-covered table, leaving an imprint of the base on the sewn-in emblem. He'd always thought the eagle had a kind of snigger.

'Guess it would be hard to. But then I'd be passing on all the knowledge stored in my head that's sat there waiting for...'

'I'm not a coach, Doc. I'm a player.'

'Was...'

'Huh?'

'You *were* a player.'

'Look, Doc. Three weeks rest and this arm will be as good as new. What do you say? Don't tell Coach, huh?'

'Mac. You're done. That arm will never pitch again.'

'I'll heal. I've always healed... and if not... give me something for the pain, will you?'

'Thought you didn't need anything...'

'Different pain, Doc. Different pain.'

Mac slid around on the bench so that his eyes could avoid being drawn to that star out there, rising and setting without him. He kept his right hand trapped between his thighs so the elbow didn't move too much.

'I can do this.'

'No, Mac. Not this time. The elbow is shot. You had so much treatment in the past the joint is calcified. No way around it. Even if you conquer the pain the joint will twist and turn and who knows what will happen to the ball.'

'That could be good. Couldn't it?'

'That could be foolish. Listen, I got to go. You coming with me?'

'No, Doc. Thanks… I need a minute.'

'Ok.'

Outside the window the dugout seats were red and hard like the new Thunderbird in last week's magazine, like the thoughts slowly filtering into Mac's brain. Coach always ranted about how he had better things to do than sit on plastic week after week getting a hard ass while watching a field full of stuffed dummies play catch out there. Now what was he going to do… join him? The light fading behind the stand etched the broken rim into stark relief, echoing the jaw of a great white. How many more players had this bowl of concrete and dust snatched up and eaten?

Mac slid off the bench and a howl of pain echoed around the small treatment room.

'Doc?'

Nothing… but the errant sound of dust settling on his career and the lost echoes of studded shoes chittering the hard floor of the corridor. Somehow he managed to stuff his right hand into the waistband of his trousers so that the pain was almost bearable. He moved forward into a world where doorknobs opened the wrong way and lift buttons were on the wrong side.

In the car lot outside, his Ford Edsel sat waiting.

'How much longer you going to sit there?'

'What else you want me to do?'

'Take out the trash would be a start.'

Mac dragged himself from the comfort of the couch and into the kitchen. With his left hand he lifted the bag of trash from the container.

'Here… I'll get the door…'

Margery leaned around him to take the handle. Mac twisted violently away. The bag ripped. Trash scattered the kitchen. Margery dropped to her knees.

'What on earth…?'

'What am I that I need your help? Tell me, huh? What am I that I can't even take out the trash single-handed?' Mac threw the remnants of the bag at her. The lid of a tin cut her face, bounced off and into the sink where it rattled around in the silence following his outburst.

'What *am* I?' he pleaded, lifting his left hand in supplication. Margery's tears picked up the blood and trickled it down her face, biblical as a river, bright and hard as the seats in the dugout.

'I don't know anymore…' she replied.

'Well at least I'm still a meal-ticket, if only a one-handed one.' He held out his right hand, the fingers trembling and shaking apart, the gaps widening and closing like shears.

'Eat out of that, can you? How much rice can you hold in there?'

'Enough for today.'

Mac shook his hand and put it back in his pocket where the trembling could continue out of his sight and he could perhaps for a minute pretend it wasn't happening.

'It's tomorrow that scares me.'

'Me too…' said Margery.

'What…why…? I thought nothing scared you. You keep telling me to go out there and find a job and not be afraid that I'll get eaten again. Do you know what it's like to be eaten alive by something? Something you can't do?'

Margery rummaged in the kitchen drawer. A piece of loose laminate caught the sleeve of her old cardigan and slapped back into place on the worktop edge as she closed it.

'Here…' she said.

'What?'

She held out the bank book.

'Look…'

He snatched the book from her. She drew her hand away as if she'd been bitten. Her shoulders set rigid, hunched and protective. The arch of her back increased until she was folding in, becoming smaller, less easy to hit and be hurt.

'What?' Mac looked at the bank book, turned it the right way around clumsily with the fingers of one hand, 'What about it?'

'The payments stopped last week.'

'That can't be right… Coach knows I'll be back soon. Another three months and I'll be ri…'

'Doc told him.'

'He promised me he wouldn't.'

'He did.'

'Shit.'

He turned the book back over and tossed it to her.

'Here… I don't want to look at it.'

'Same old, same old…'

Margery began to gather up the trash, scooping the dark squalid mess together with her hands.

'Don't you do that while I'm here!' Mac leaned over her, his body twisting from inside where rage nested and incubated, dark as the pool of trash, 'Don't you use both hands like that in front of me…'

Margery looked up.

'Go back to your film, hon. Sometimes I forget I'm supposed to understand.'

'What's that supposed to mean?'

Margery ignored him and corralled the trash into a corner using only her left hand.

'See! Now you know what it's like.'

'No, hon… I don't. I only know it's awkward. It's not eating me up. It's just… difficult. Something I have to get over.'

'That's stupid. Don't talk to me that way. I only want back what I had… is that too much to ask, huh?'

'No, hon,' Margery turned over and sat on the floor, her back against the sink, 'Just don't always expect an answer, that's all I want to say.'

Mac pointed at the bank book she'd left on the floor beside her.

'What you going to do about that?'

'Might as well go in the trash.'

'No. What you going to do about having no money?'

'I'll get a job…'

'No you won't. I'll go see Doc and get some more of those painkillers. Coach'll let me play again if Doc says so.'

'No, hon, he won't. A letter came with the last payment.'

'Letter? I haven't seen no letter.'

'It was addressed to me.'

'I still should've seen it. Where is it?'

'In the trash.'

'Where?'

Margery stretched herself up from the floor and slid past his anger into the room beyond where the television flickered it's subliminal life away in a stream of adverts for things they could no longer afford.

Parts were getting difficult to find for the Edsel since Ford had realised that no-one was buying and if it broke down again she would have to shop local instead of going to the

Mart and everyone knew how expensive that was and suddenly it struck her with a laugh how ridiculous that sounded. If you don't have any money it doesn't matter where you shop. You might as well eat gold-plated if all you're doing is exercising your imagination instead of your teeth.

'What you laughing at?' Mac demanded from the kitchen.' He scrabbled around one-handed in the trash pile until his fingers closed around a folded piece of paper. His skin could sense the desperation in the way that it was crushed.

Margery called in from the tentative safety of the sitting-room doorway, 'Have you ever heard of 'Irony'?'

Mac snapped back, 'Put down the crossword. I think I found the letter.'

He struggled into the place Margery had just left, the sink base cold against his back through the thin summer shirt he wore all year.

'Dear Margery...' Mac's face twisted into a snarl, his skin, once dark from hours on the open practice field, folding into creases as stained and white-edged as the letter in his good left hand.

'When did he... What' they doing writing to you?'

'Because when they write to you, you throw them straight in the trash because you're afraid to open them. Because it might be this one. Because they all were but you won't listen to nobody.'

'Calm down... calm down...' he shook a wrinkle out of the paper... a slice of peeled onion hit the wall and slid slowly down. Margery watched it leaving a trail, as if the snail of her life the last three months was slithering inexorably downwards into the pile of trash.

' 'Dear Margery'... at least they spelled your name right... 'it is with regret that I have to tell you that the insurance payments have reached an end.'…bastards… How much have I paid into that Plan, I ask you… how much?'

Margery was fixated by the onion slipping down the wall… Mac went on…

'What?… 'Because Doc lied to the Insurance it has made it possible to continue to pay Injury Benefit for the last three months but now they are asking questions. I hope you can convince Mac to keep quiet if they come around.' What does he think I am? Some kind of dummy? What about my lump sum payoff? Hey? Where's that?'

Margery, emboldened by the sudden static stuttering of the TV in the corner shouted back.

'It's in the trash!'

Mac stared at her through the opening, wondering what had happened to this once-blonde, slender emblem of his successful career. Was any of that left, hiding behind the faded summer print working shirt and the jeans now stained at the knees with the dark ooze of the trashcan? Maybe if he looked hard… but the harder he looked, the more he could see of himself.

'What are you talking about?'

'In the trash. What else do you have there?'

Mac cast around him as far as his left arm would reach, looking for something that would make sense of her words.

'Nothing… Utility bills… repairs to the car… City taxes… grocery bills… Nothing.'

'That's about the size of it. Nothing. That's where it went.'

'How can you spend all our money on things like that. How do we eat?'

'You already ate most of it. You still eat like you were in training. Look at you!'

Mac caught sight of himself in the reflection from the glass door of the stove. A growing paunch hung over the belt of his trousers. His chin was in the process of doubling, no… trebling. He fingered the unshaven whiskers.

'OK. I could ease off a little.'

'You can ease off a lot. All we have is in the fridge.'

Mac eased himself up the side of the unit and opened the fridge door. The chill air spilled over him like the breath of a premonition.

'Two pints of milk, half a loaf of bread… tin of sardines… three tomatoes.. that's about the size of it… throw in a few more fish and a Bible, we could have a regular feast.'

The Edsel slid backwards out of the garage. Mac leaned over and pulled up the brake with his left hand but the drive was steep and the car continued to roll down and onto the road. He swung the wheel dramatically with one hand and managed to keep it close to the kerb. He hit the start button and the engine dragged into a knocking, rattling frenzy. He twisted around, nudged it into drive and parked it at the bottom of the lawn. Margery leaned out from under the garage door.

'Mac? What you doing? You Ok?'

'I'm cleaning the car, Margery. Is that Ok?'

Margery turned back into the dark cover of the garage.

Mac heard her shout, 'I'll ask my brother to fix the TV tomorrow…' before the door slammed shut behind her.

Mac struggled his hand into the glovebox and pulled out the bunch of papers he had hidden there the week before. He dropped them in his lap and sifted through them slowly, counting up the numbers at the bottom of the sheets until he got to the total. He breathed in, then out again slowly…

-$2800… his net worth. He'd had the house valued and offset the mortgage, including the extra interest on non/late payment as the accountant called it, against the sale price, and come up with negative equity. The Bank was overdrawn to another six hundred and they owed money to the car shop, taxes... you name it. He punched at the horn on the Edsel wheel... but only managed to shift the gear. He pulled up the last piece of paper and read it again, very, very carefully, taking great care to check even the spelling of every word and meaning that might be hidden behind what it actually said. Satisfied, he stuffed it into the pocket of his shirt and got out of the car.

In the kitchen, Margery stood fascinated by the trail the onion had left down the wall the day of the argument. For some unknown reason she couldn't bring herself to clean it off. After the argument with Mac she'd stood there, like this, and watched until the onion had finally reached the pile where it became just another layer of trash like all the days of her life since Mac stopped playing.

Exhausted by the thoughts that flickered her head as if she was some old TV on standby, the tiny impulses that drove her sprang to life then were extinguished before they had a chance to become reality. They had become little more than sporadic ions, brief as dreams and as quickly dissipated. She moved to the sink and plunged her hands into hard, cold water. The shock opened her senses to the hiss of the pipes as Mac turned on the hose inside the garage.

Outside, Mac reeled the hose out to the roadside. He led it over the front of the car to where the vertical grille glared at him in reflected, baleful fury.

'I hate you, too,' he thought, draping the hose in an almost accidental fashion over and around a rear wheel, anchoring the end with the nozzle under the closed lid of the trunk. He picked up a slack length and felt it under his thumb, the water pressure made the plastic hard and unforgiving. He nodded and dropped it to the floor.

Inside the garage, the hose rose up as it entered the door and ran horizontally over two roof timbers then descended again towards the back where it was anchored to a tap fixed firmly to the wall. Mac jumped up at full stretch and pulled down a section of hose in the centre of the two beams. He trapped it under his right armpit and managed to throw a double loop into the length. He placed a heavy wrench into the loop to hold it to the floor while he went back down to the car.

Mac sat himself firmly in the driving seat, hating this car in the way he had ever since he'd bought it. He recalled thinking how clever it had seemed. He knew they'd be a short run. Not everyone liked the style and it was such a departure that soon, if he could keep it for a few years, it would become a collector's item.

Somehow that Edsel represented every investment he'd ever made. He sat there a moment then, without knowing why, began to kick at the pedals. He punched the wheel, the radio, the dash, the speedometer, tore his nails against the upholstery, screamed at the windshield, but nothing changed. The car, implacable as ever, continued silently sinking out of sight in his sea of unimaginably poor investment, becoming another rock in the financial debris against which he continually barked his shins. He released the handbrake and the hose took up the slack.

The street outside was a slight slope, hardly worth the name, little more than one or two degrees, but Mac figured it should be enough. He slammed the door with a final fury. In the kitchen, Margery felt the slam as if it had rattled the windows and the pots on the shelf, but didn't dare turn around.

Back in the shade of the garage, Mac picked up the double loop he'd made and widened it. He pulled it over his head and took up the tension. He felt the cold of the water seeping into his neck, into fragile muscles and frail tendons. With his good arm he reached up to the length of hose beyond the loop and tugged hard.

The hose unwound from around the rear wheel where it had held the tyre fixed to the spot. Mac waited impatiently for gravity to take over. Outside on the street, the Edsel began its fatal journey. Slowly, the wheels began to turn. Chips of asphalt made way for rubber, spitting out sideways under pressure, tyre marks imprinting in the sun-warmed pitch. The hose loosened imperceptibly as the car crept silently past the end of the drive, gathering speed and momentum. By the time it had travelled twenty feet more the collected energy lifted the hose clear of the path. Mac watched it as if it were alive then suddenly it straightened and yanked him off his feet leaving him flailing in the air, feet jerking and kicking, tearing at his neck with one good hand in a last moment of regret.

As he struggled, the life insurance document fell out of his shirt pocket into a vivid black pool of oil left by the Edsel on the garage floor. Calmer, as the oxygen was leaving his brain, he saw the light bulb dim and the daylight fade beyond the door. As the blackness overtook him his knees banged painfully into something hard and red.

When Mac awoke, the only things mobile were his eyes. He stared at the ceiling trying to recognise something, a patch of damp, a flake of paint... anything that would identify where he was. Light crept in from the corner at high level. Maybe that was a clue. He had a vague memory from behind his eyelids as though someone had leaned over him, obscuring the light. Off to his right a brightness was echoing off the wall but somehow his head was clamped into this position. He heard the bright clatter of instruments in a metal tray…

'Jesus…' he thought, 'I'm in the morgue.'

He tried to speak but his lips wouldn't move. His eyes would only describe a tiny arc and all he could glean were the sounds of metal on metal and the softer underlying ruffle of cloth. Straining as hard as he might, over to the right of where he lay he could sense rather than see a moving shadow, perhaps no more than a darker shade in the brightness there.

He laid back and waited for the sharp sensation of the knife that he knew would start deep in the folds of his neck and continue describing a bloodless line all the way through his sternum, his peritoneal cavity, until it met the hardness of his pubic bone. He wondered if he would cry out, or if this was what it felt like to be dead. But if he was dead, why would he still be able to hear? Christ, this was another mistake. He was as inept as Margery had said that day in the kitchen.

He gathered his remaining wind into his throat and pushed. He heard a soft croak fall into the air around his ears and realised that it was the sound he himself had made. He tried again but there was nothing left within him for his vocal chords to gain a purchase on. He relaxed… and waited to die… again. Perhaps this was better than he had imagined. The insurance company couldn't argue this if it turned out that the pathologist had killed him. Margery would be safe. And so would the little lump that, laid here, he could almost feel growing and stretching inside her, soon to be kicking her awake in the middle of the night. He felt tears overflow his eyes and trickle down his face. Awareness. Awareness returning. He'd felt the tears. Try again… 'croak'… CROAK.'

He collapsed into himself, exhausted by the effort. He swivelled his eyes as far as they would go. The shadow, no, the space within the bright light, was stilled.

'You awake in there, Mac?'

Mac didn't recognise the voice, but it sounded solid, and somehow competent. It was a useful voice. And it knew his name... He let it soothe him and slow his heart rate until the panic went away. The Devil would be harsher than that, especially now that he had him. He managed a small grunt by way of acknowledgement.

'It doesn't matter. Try not to move for a minute.'

Mac grunted involuntarily.

As his consciousness returned his skin came alive with an awareness he'd not noticed before. Underneath him was a cotton sheet, he could feel the weave imprinting his skin, and beneath that... was the stitching that he knew was formed into an eagle.

'Doc...' he managed.

'Yeah, I'm a Doc,' came the voice again, 'but not the one you think. Be quiet a minute. I'm working.'

Mac closed his eyes and relaxed again. As the darkness fell behind his lids he thought he could feel someone tugging at his arm... in fact... at his damaged elbow. A voice cut across him as he lay there trying to imagine what was happening. And this time he recognised it.

'Coach?' he managed.

A hand touched his shoulder lightly. He could sense the tremble in it that meant Coach had gone at least eight hours without a drink. The fingers tapped him gently in recognition. He smiled and gave himself up to whatever was happening.

Coach would never let him down. No matter what.

A vibrant buzz filled the room as a tremor filled his arm and shoulder, then a smell... like burning bone. Jesus! They were amputating!

'Wha...!' was all he could manage.

'His heart rate jumped again. It's sky-high... is that the blood pressure?'

'Yeah, that one there with the silver stuff in.'

The other voice still seemed laconic, laid back to beyond the centre of gravity that Mac could sense in Coach. Coach's hand left his shoulder.

'He's waking up.'

'Ok. We'll let him wake up. He's panicking in there about what we're doing anyway. Can't afford to lose him now.'

'Thought you said that was impossible?' Coach's voice had adopted the same tremor that his fingers had displayed.

'No, I said it was improbable.'

'Then wake him up. He needs to know.'

'Ok. You're the Coach.'

Mac felt a needle slide silently and without pain into his neck. There was a sensation of utter cold, then his brain began to clear. A hand slipped under his head and lifted him gently into a slightly raised position. The first thing he saw from there was his right arm, disconnected at the elbow, with his forearm and hand dangling by skin and cords and tendons. His upper arm was supported in a shaped block that fitted neatly up to his armpit. A tall, dark-haired man in protective glasses and theatre smock smiled knowingly at him. Mac couldn't take his eyes off the circular saw in his hand long enough to return it.

'Here...' the man picked up a piece of raw white bone from a small stand beside him. 'Look at this.'

'Wha... what is it?'

'It's your elbow... or what's left of it. Look...'

He took hold of the bone at each side of the joint and tugged lightly. The joint came apart with a sick, sucking sound. Mac gagged.

'Don't worry,' the man said calmly, 'it's only redundant connective tissue. Here… this is what I want to show you.'

He exposed the inner surfaces of the joint. Mac could see that there were spurs growing on the inner surface and that these had worn away any pretence of lubricating tissue there might once have been.

'There you go…' said the man, 'that's what pain looks like in the flesh, so to speak.'

'Please…' said Mac, 'don't cut it off. Even if it doesn't work I…'

'Hold on,' the man said, putting the broken joint back into the dish on the stand. 'I have something else to show you.'

Behind him was a tall cabinet like the ones they had in the car shop, but this one was bright red and polished, like the T Bird in the magazine and had a label on it that read 'Snap-On'. The man opened it and reached in as a small surge of frigid air escaped the lid. It tainted the room with the faint scent of antiseptic. He took out a parcel wrapped in a fine film of sheer plastic that Mac had never seen before.

Watching it unravel, Mac almost forgot about what was in it. The man held a cylindrically shaped piece of jointed metal into the light where it reflected brightly.

'What is it?' Mac's vocal chords were gathering strength as the injection fed through his entire body, bringing back all his sensations except pain.

'It's your new elbow. Look…' The man twisted it around and it shone in gold and white and the movement was silent and smooth and…

'What's it made of?' said Mac

'Gold plated rhodium and silicone.'

'Will it work?'

The man smiled,

'Trust me. I'm a Doctor,' he said, as a second needle slid into Mac's neck.

'Mac?'

'Margery?'

Mac opened his eyes into the bright light streaming through a gap in the closed bedroom curtains. He knew instantly that he was home. He'd bought those curtains himself a year ago. They were too short then and he'd refused to take them back. So he told Margery he liked the gap. It meant they could keep an eye on the neighbourhood, even while they were asleep, so they could see if it was running down... or something. Margery had shrugged and climbed into bed, pulling the covers over her head

'The neighbourhood can also keep an eye on us...' she'd said, 'See if we're running down... or something.'

'Some chance...' he'd replied. But now he was glad to see them, too short or not.

'How do you feel, Mac.'

'Coach?'

'Yeah.'

'I don't know... I don't know how I feel.'

'You'll be fine in a day or two.' This voice belonged, he remembered, to the Doctor. He tried to turn his head but the pain had returned to everywhere in his body it seemed. The skin around his neck was stinging like a third degree burn and his right arm was a source of pale fire tightly strapped to the ribs on that side. The Doctor stepped around the bed so that Mac could see him.

'Did... did it work, Doc?'

'Yep. Good as new. Well, in a week, maybe a month... or two.' He looked sideways at the coach, 'You got the date, right?'

Coach patted his jacket pocket.

'Written down. Square as you like.'

Margery pushed her way between them.

'What is this? Can't you let him rest? Look what he's been through.'

'Margery...' the Doctor said.

'Who are you? Who are you to call me Margery? I don't know you. I don't even know your name.'

'And that's how it will stay, I'm afraid,' the Doctor said, 'Now, Coach and I need a few minutes alone with Mac.'

Mac looked at them all. Throughout this he knew where Coach stood, even though he didn't know who or even what the Doctor was, and if Coach let him operate on Mac's arm, that was good enough for Mac. He nodded to Margery.

'Oh, Mac...'

He nodded again. Margery closed the kitchen door behind her.

'Coach, pull up the chair. Doc? Can you open the curtains a little please?'

The Doctor drew the curtains right back and turned to see the reaction on Mac's face. Apart from a slight squint in the brightness of the day, he seemed alright. He came and sat on the bed as the sun clouded over outside and the light fell in the room. Mac relaxed a little more.

'Ok, what's this all about? Are you sent by the Insurance?'

'You could say that,' replied the Doctor. Coach shook his head as Mac turned to him,

'Sorry Mac, I don't know myself. But I should listen to what he has to say. I listened to him, and though I don't agree with everything...' he cast a look towards the Doctor sat at the other side of the bed, '...I decided I could square it with my conscience.'

'Fire away then, Doc.'

'Alright Mac. Have you heard of 'OmiGor Gum'?'

'Who hasn't. What's that got to do with the price of eggs?'

'Remember the photographer who came around... when was it Coach?'

'Around six months ago. Did the team pictures... you remember, Mac.'

'Yeah, I remember. So what? Is he paying for this?'

The Doctor laughed out loud.

'You could say that.'

Mac tried to push himself into a sitting position with one arm. Coach got up and lifted him gently and shook out the pillows.

'Listen, Doc. I'm getting kind of tired here, and there's only so long I can keep Margery in the kitchen. God knows she spends long enough in there.'

'Ok.' Doc waited until Coach sat down again.

'The photographer, without the knowledge of the Coach here... sold the pictures to OmiGor Gum.'

'So now they have a team picture. So what. So do half the kids in town.'

The Doctor smoothed the bedcover with one hand. Mac watched the slender but strong fingers iron out the creases.

'They also had the individual pictures of the players.'

'Big deal.'

'Maybe not now. But it will be. You see, OmiGor used the pictures on their bubble-gum cards.'

'So I'm famous...'

'No, not yet.'

'So now they owe me some money. Is that it? And they sent you to fix me up and buy me off? Huh, Coach? Is that the long and short of it?'

Coach shook his head slowly.

'Nope. It ain't that easy. Wait and listen.'

'Ok, Doc. I'm all ears. Go ahead.'

'While you've been wallowing around in self-pity and driving Margery to distraction, the OmiGor Gum factory burned down.'

Mac narrowed his eyes at the Doctor.

'How come you know all this?'

'Because I torched it.'

'What!'

'I torched it. The whole place. Went up in the sweetest smoke you ever did smell. Burned for three days. All the firemen were on a sugar high.'

'Why would a Doctor do that? What kind of a Doctor are you?'

'Orthopaedic Surgeon, actually. And a rich one at that.'

'Then how come I get your service for free?'

'Oh no, Mac. It's not for free. There's something you have to do to make it work.'

Mac slumped back down in the bed,

'Ok. I know… sort of… what these things oughta cost. Who do I have to kill?'

'Nobody.'

'Nobody?'

'That's right. Nobody.'

'Ok. Let's hear it…'

'It's simple. All you have to do is to take this…' he held out something like a playing card wrapped in the same sheer plastic that had covered the joint, '…and slip it behind the door liner, passenger side, of your old Edsel.'

'That's it? Then what happens to it?' Mac began to unravel the plastic. It stuck to his fingers but there seemed to be no glue on it,

'What on earth is this stuff?'

'It's called… never mind. You'll see a lot of it in the future.'

By now, Mac had unwrapped the card.

'Hey look! It's me. Hey Marge...?'

'Shush.' Coach clamped a hand over Mac's mouth.

Mac's eyes bulged in their sockets from the suppressed yell but he quietened down and Coach removed his hand.

They waited a moment but the kitchen door remained firmly closed. Inside, Margery was staring fixedly at the onion stain, wondering why she could never seem to pluck up the courage to wipe it off.

The Doctor took the card back and wrapped it again very carefully, sealing the edges with an easy pressure between finger and thumb,

'You must do exactly as I say or this won't work. For any of us.'

Mac shrugged, 'Ok.'

'Here's how it goes...' the Doctor shuffled himself into a more comfortable position on the bed, 'In time, these bubble-gum cards will be worth a lot of money.'

'The kids swap them for peanuts down at the lot.'

Coach touched his shoulder and nodded him to silence.

'More money,' the Doctor said, 'than you can imagine right now.'

'There are milli...'

'I know, there are millions of them right now. But there won't be. They'll get burned up in house fires, thrown out with the trash when the kids think they're too old to collect stupid things like bubble-gum cards. But then, those self-same kids will grow up. They'll start to wonder what they had in life way back then and to wonder why they lost it. Some of them will have more money than they know what to do with and one day, they'll be back there down that lot swapping these cards again. But this time it won't be for peanuts. Do you know how much an early Mickey Mantle or a Sandy Koufax fetches?'

'Who's he?'

The Doctor thought for a moment, then laughed, mostly to himself,

'Wait around a while, you'll find out. Anyway, let's just say that it's an awful amount of money.'

'And this one?' asked Mac, holding up the card.

'It's worth three of each of the others together.' The Doctor unwrapped the card again and handed it back to Mac.

'Handle it carefully. Don't crease it or get finger marks on it. Hold it by the edge. That's right. Now read the back.'

Mac held it into the light.

'Says here '...Mac never made it into the Majors. Best up-and-coming pitcher for three years running then invalided out of the game with a broken elbow...' What good is that?'

'The card is wrong. Do you know how many cashiered players ever made it back into the game? No? One. That's you.'

Mac looked at Coach. Coach smiled back and nodded.

'I have the date here, squared away in my pocket.' He tapped his jacket.

'I don't believe this,' said Mac, 'I still don't believe I don't have to kill somebody.'

The Doctor took the card gently from his fingers and held it up into the light.

'Do you know how many of these there are? No? I'll tell you. One. I burned the rest. Do you know what that makes this? Unique.'

'And you're going to give it me... for what? It ain't worth a hill of beans in this town. It might be where you come from, but who's interested in the lower leagues?'

'You are going to put this card into the door liner of your Edsel like I said. Then, you're going to drive it one last time into the rear of the garage, put it up on bricks and leave it there.'

'Then what do I drive?'

'Don't worry, we brought you a new car,' said Coach.

'Ok. What do I have to do to earn it?'

'That's easy,' said the Doctor, 'Just play ball.'

'I don't get this yet, there's something here you aren't letting on about.'

'Look,' the Doctor said, 'In around fifty years, I buy the Edsel from your son.'

'My... my son?' Mac's eyes filled with tears, 'My... son. Doc? How good does that sound? Hey, don't tell Margery. She's says she knows she's having a girl.'

'She's only teasing. Anyways, by the time he's fifty you'll be freshly gone and planted and he'll be stood there out on the street and scratching his head and wondering what the hell to do with this old place you neither sold nor rented out and I'll come along and give him the best price ever for it.'

'You will? I mean, you wouldn't gyp him or anything?'

'No. Or the whole thing collapses like a house of cards. You see, I have a hobby... a paradox tucked somewhere between Physics and Philosophy. Only thing it needed to make it work was the money.'

'And it works?'

'I'm here, aren't I?'

'Ok... I'll do it.' Mac turned around whichever way he could for best, smiles wreathing his face, his breath caught in the middle of wonder and decision, coming soft and then hard, 'By God. I'll do it... My son, eh? How does that sound? What's he like, Doc?'

'Just like you. Gives his wife a hard time.'

'Margery! She has to know!'

'No, Mac. She can never know. You'll have to take the flak for keeping the old Edsel tucked away and be quiet about it. Don't worry, it'll be good for your soul.'

Mac lifted one foot from the floor, screwed his body until he was coiled like a human spring. He hesitated. Lifted one finger from the ball, then quickly another two. He turned his head to the right. Margery was there somewhere, lost in the sea of faces in the new stand. Without looking, he spun around and unleashed the ball. He knew exactly where it was going. The new elbow had no shake or shudder like the old one. The Catcher took it full on and staggered back off field. Mac nodded and waited for the ball to come back. He plucked it from the air and in a moment of supreme fluidity swung it around in an arc towards third base, hitting the plate square on.

He saw Coach leap up from the seat in the dugout, the bright plaid cushions screaming contrast. He looked up at the scoreboard and for once, the eagle seemed to be smiling.

Mac walked out to the car lot after everyone else had left. His was the only car there… but he would have known it anywhere, that red T Bird with the scuffed hood.

He pulled into the drive and Margery opened the garage door. They were moving house next week. Coach had sold him into the Majors and pocketed a nice fat fee in the process, just the way the Doctor had said he would.

They'd keep this house on. He'd visit here once in a while and sit there in front of the old TV that didn't work and be grateful for what little he knew. Margery could come in and stare at that old onion stain until she could pluck up the courage to turn her back on it and walk away again.

He pulled the T Bird up the drive and under the shade of the canopy. He got out of the car and closed the door behind him. On his way through to the house he patted the fender of the Edsel.

Best damned investment he ever made.

Red-Stripe Candy

Is Red-Stripe Candy what it seems? I'm not sure. Maybe it started out as one kind of a story and became another. I wrote this in a period when I was obsessed with becoming the next Ray Bradbury until I learned that there is only one Ray Bradbury, as there is only one Bill Allerton, unless you count the several other very successful ones I Googled around the world in the USA, Canada and Australia, to name but a few.

There's also one who runs a Record Store in London. (I keep being asked if that's me. Fortunately for him, I'm not…) Some of the others have been so successful that I'm beginning to feel I'm letting the side down…

Occasionally I write in what can only be (charitably) described as a mid-western voice. No, I have no idea where it comes from except that I find it incredibly easy to adopt. Perhaps the fact that an Edward (my middle name) Allerton was a passenger on The Mayflower in 1620, as was Patience, his daughter. I always say that she took all the patience genes with her, and that explains my intolerance…

Red-Stripe Candy embodies some of my favourite themes, Time, relationships, the harbouring of dark and unrequited pain, inequality and steam trains. Okay, strange bedfellows you might say, but there is something to savour in all of these things. Even if they prove no more substantial than steam, they are the forces that drive us.

Red-Stripe Candy

'Libby!'

Virna Morrell occupies the corner by the slatted french window like a jewelled ornament shrouded in black lace. When she speaks, only her lips move, only her breath scatters motes in the bracketed light.

'Comin' Miss Virna.'

Libby's voice carries in from the kitchen on a wave of cooking smells. There is cabbage, and all kinds of green stuff cut fresh from a garden now hemmed by weeds and brought closer to the house by each season.

'Hey, Libby!'

'Yes, Miss Virna.'

'Libby! It's almost two o'clock.'

'Comin', Miss Virna.'

The clock in the hall starts its groan as Libby pulls herself through from the kitchen. In the drawing room, each piece of furniture waits to fall under her familiar hand.

'Better than Kin,' she would always say, 'At least you knows where it stands!'

Libby brakes the wheels on Miss Virna's chair with a foot she can hardly see for the swelling in her ankles. She straightens the bright-flowered print of her frock with one hand and with the other she pushes back a stray lock of starlit black hair and wipes the pain from her face.

'Now then, Miss Virna. What you wanna see today?'

'The train, Libby. The train.'

'Just the old milk run, Miss Virna, t'aint nuthin' special.'

Virna remains silent, her eyes fixed on the slats of the right hand shutter where it hangs, waiting for the years in Libby's gnarled and broken hands to shake the rust from the hinges.

'If I opens the other side, p'raps we'll see the Reverend and his pretty wife in their new car. You knows they always wave an'… the way her face lits up a dull day! Like your sister you say, back in '34. But Abby would've been 'bout thirty then and this one cain't be no more than, oh, twenty three or so, and her with them two kids runnin' round like peas in a pod…'

Virna's gaze remains fixed on the right hand shutter. If she sits perfectly still, like a dark butterfly resting… all folded wings and withdrawn, inwardly-directed senses… then at two o'clock each day between mid-May and August… on days when the sky is open and wide, not closed and shuttered and dark with clouds like this room in which she sits… the sun will chip sparks from the gold on her fingers and shimmer the inlaid silver and mother-of-pearl around her throat. Her head will lean forwards and a little to one side, and she will smile her only smile in the shadow of Libby's relentless chatter.

'…an' when the clock strikes we can watch it shower the old-town with doves, an' some o' them dirty grey pigeons they seem to've taken up with. Cain't say I like grey. Was grey the

day I buried my daddy. Was grey the day I got the letter sayin'
my Joseph weren't never comin' back an' it's grey when I look
in the mirror. And the pain! Some people say pain's red. But I
tell you it ain't so. Pain's grey!'

'The train, Libby.'

'Yes Ma'am Miss Virna.'

'Can't help but see the church whichever way I look,
Libby.'

'Yes Ma'am Miss Virna. The train it is. Choo Choo.'

'Shut up, Libby.'

'Yes Ma'am… Miss Virna.'

Outside the french windows the air falls still, like the
world holding its breath and waiting for summer to steal in
unannounced, the ground barely dry from last nights shower.
Beyond a quarter acre of grass stands a row of tall cypress
trees, their flame shapes casting fine, filigreed shadows over
the lawn.

Hemmings planted them in his fiftieth year so that Miss
Virna didn't have to see the way that the houses and sheds
and streets and the bus station had crept steadily up towards
the old house. As the town grew, the trees stretched up and
wide as if conspiring to keep the worst of the days from her.
Now, they filter the street noises from the air, and when the
wind blows they bend with an old-fashioned grace to protect
the shingle roof.

Seen from beyond the hedge the house is enigmatic,
something of an anachronism. It looms like an elder sister
over the small, white, clapboard church at the bottom of the
drive as though they are locked… religion just a curve away
from tradition… a slow crunch of gravel apart.

Virna understands that journey almost as well as she
understands herself. It feels like yesterday, but it's a journey
she hasn't made in twenty-five years.

To the right of the church, over by a street of low black-pitch-roofed garages and kiosks, stands the Station. Its gable roof is canted so high above the tracks that on hot days the sun slides under and around it so that it's mostly no use at all. The broad white gingerbread fascias were once lovingly re-painted every two years by Jackson, the retired engine driver come Station Master, porter, painter... well, almost anything that needed doing... but now his broken ladder frames the flowers that grow in a twenty-foot bed behind the platform.

From the office window Jackson can see the old house, and although from his chair he can't see her... not like forty years or so ago, when he could've counted the birds in the hedgerow and admired the slim, brown stretch of Miss Libby's legs as she tidied the garden... he can still imagine that Miss Virna, punctual as ever, is sitting behind one shutter and peering out through the other where it swings wide on the world.

He had once asked her why she didn't just throw them both open and have done.

'Too much world at once, Mr Jackson,' she had said, 'I don't think I was made for that much world at once.'

She never had called him to the house again, and sometimes it felt as though he'd just sat back to watch the dust settle on and around her.

From the side of a rail baking in the early summer heat, a flake of rust falls into the gravel bed. The iron sings softly to itself and the station cat opens one slow, haunted eye.

Jackson takes a last look up the hill towards Miss Virna in her chair, in her prison, in her own time. Around him, the Station waits, open mouthed, dust settling quietly on its fifteen-year paintwork.

'Say, Libby?'

'Yes'm?'

'I was just 'minded of red-stripe candy.'

'Now there's a thing.'

Virna scowls at the implied sarcasm, 'The train's late.'

'No, Ma'am. Clock's fast. Church ain't struck yet.'

Virna listens lightly for the urgent throb of the diesel engine entering the ravine, her thoughts running barefoot, 'Red-stripe candy.'

'Yes'm?'

'The preacher's boys. I swear they smelled of red-stripe candy. You remember, the kind that's all spirals of white and red and peppermint taste and bent at the end like a walking stick? I could smell it for hours after they'd gone.'

She sniffs the air sharply.

'There! Still a trace. Just a trace though, it's fading now. Can't you smell it Libby?'

'No Ma'am. I sure cain't. Them boys haven't been here in years.'

'Libby! They were here just the other day.'

'No Ma'am. Sure as I'm here.'

'You're getting old, Libby.'

'Sure am, Miss Virna. From haulin' you around in that damn chair.'

Though familiar, Libby's remark passes across Virna's thoughts like a dark hand. She has felt old for almost as long as she can remember, except for that one time... and that one time had made the scar that left her in this chair and waiting for a darker comfort.

'Libby!'

'Yes, Miss Virna?'

'My best shawl.'

'Company comin'?'

'Don't know, Libby. I just know I need my best shawl.'

Libby negotiates the furniture to the hallway. From there, she sits at the bottom of the stairs and shuffles her way up, one step at a time.

From behind the closed left shutter Virna's eyes pierce the distance until they blur upon the open mouth of the Station. The church clock hangs at a few minutes to two. The chimes of the hall clock are five long minutes gone, pushed by silence into the all too easily forgotten past.

Libby pauses at the top of the stairs to catch her breath and allow the pounding in her body to subside. Through the silence of the house, she listens to the drum of occluded arteries in her head.

Hemmings is outside tidying the kitchen garden, stoking the mulch back around the cabbages where Libby used to stump between the rows, looking for the best of the early ones. The afternoon sun is warm on his back, easing tomorrow's pain from his muscles. As he works his way along the side of the house to where the garden is edged by lawn, he stops to light his pipe.

Earlier this morning the wind had sighed gently through the cypress trees, trimming their leaves towards the house, trapping within themselves the sounds of cars and children and the clang and shut of businesses kept at bay by the sheer presence of the old house, but now there is silence. The air is still, as if the world and it's neighbour are on vacation and he alone is left with a chance to relax and edge the lawn in peace without the sounds of dogs barking... or the smell of barbecued grease clinging to his summer shirt.

Enjoying the moment, Hemmings sits by the edge of the lawn, pipe warm in his cupped hand, the uneven charcoal rim dark against the slow fire of his memories.

Upstairs, Libby lifts Miss Virna's best shawl to her face and breathes in through the black Parisienne lace. It holds a faint but pervasive scent of peppermint. It lingers in her mind as she stretches the cloth over her fingers to rub at the coarseness of its weave with her thumb, feeling the patterns under her skin and experiencing the darkness within the folds.

Going down the stairs will be easier with lungs that don't ache and a chest that doesn't pound and a head that is more silent than hers right now, so she sits on the edge of the bed for a while, enveloped in the peppermint scent from the shawl.

The church clock strikes a knell into the warmth of the mid-afternoon. Doves rocket out from the belfry louvres and settle with the grace of confetti on the surrounding outhouse roofs. Miss Virna watches them dispassionately from a corner of her eye while she times the coming of the second knell with precision. The clapboard sides and the quarter-paned windows of the house take the sound with an easy grace.

'It's late, Libby.'

Libby is taking the stairs one step at a time, the shawl thrown across her own shoulders and shaming the crystal grey of her hair.

Virna's eyes never waver from the gaping mouth of the Station roof.

'Libby! Libby! Where is that girl?'

Libby stumps from the hat rack to the calling-card table by the hall door.

'Pray tell where should I be, Miss Virna?'

'Right here. By me. Where you belong.'

Libby drapes the shawl across Miss Virna's shoulders, adjusting the length against the chair back.

'I swear some days I don't know who belongs where or to what 'cept I wouldn't care if only these legs belonged somebody else that's all 'cept I cain't think of anybody I hates that much 'cept…'

'Shut up, Libby.'

'Yes Ma'am, Miss Virna.'

'The train's late, Libby.'

'Yes Ma'am, Miss Virna.'

The room shakes to the gentle thunder of a train travelling the ravine that separates the house from the suburban sprawl to the east. Miss Virna nods satisfactorily as if the coming of the train has turned a chapter in her book, or maybe marked the ever-shortening calendar in her head.

Out by the mulch bin, Hemmings coughs in a sudden pall of dark smoke that billows up from the divide. He hears the throttle eased as the train sleee-s to a halt in the Station.

Jackson jumps up with a bound he had lately thought beyond all expectation. The cat cowers beneath a trolley, away from the shooting, reaching, twisting steam and the hiss and sudden heat of hot black iron. Jackson closes his eyes to sniff the air. It's a steamer alright, a 4-6-2 Pacific on a high-slung frame with super-heat and double acting cylinders, just like the one that finished his days and still screams its way through his dreams of a night, but what the hell is it doing here in all its black-spit an' brass-polish glory?

So far beyond human scale, the engine is magnificent, and monstrously alive. The driving wheels are wider than Jackson could span with both arms and in the places where they have met the steel rails they are polished with the sheen of a thousand, thousand miles. The footplate is empty. He steps up.

His lungs fill with the scent of tar bubbling from the seams in the swelling coals where they stir, bursting fire and flame under the boiler. He climbs back down to the platform where the taste of hot grease oozing from the axle boxes and brake trunnions is a tangible thing. He takes a breath of steam, and feels it invades his tissues like the first faint tang of peppermint.

Behind the night-black of the engine the silent carriages shimmer mid-brown in the sunlight. A gold inlay runs at waist height on a line through the handles. On tiptoe, Jackson peers through the first window. It is dark inside and at first seems empty, but as he looks he thinks to see movement, then dismisses it as steam wisping the glass.

Along the platform he hears the snick of a brass coach-handle. A door swings wide to show rich leather upholstery. A man steps down beside the track. He speaks quietly, and with the ease of familiarity.

'Hello, Roy.'

Libby takes the chair by Miss Virna and curves her spine against the high back. Virna sits watching the Station mouth spill and overflow with cotton-candy clouds.

'Say, Libby? Is the Station afire?'

'Cain't say for sure, Miss Virna. I b'lieve it might be.'

'Look! There's Jackson comin' up the hill. Who's the young man with him?'

'Cain't say, Miss Virna, your eyes better'n mine. You been savin' yours an' usin' mine for years.'

'Now, Libby!'

'Yes Ma'am, Miss Virna.'

Roy Jackson takes the first fifty feet of the hill with a deceptive ease, but he stops there to shake the hand of a smartly dressed young man and to wave him on up to the old house. The man takes the next fifty yards before he begins to slow. Roy notices the left leg take on a cautious swing that turns gradually into a well-defined limp as he walks on. Twitching forward as the man stumbles, Roy relaxes again as he rights himself and carries on up the hill, a little more stooped now than before. Past the halfway mark, the man pauses to push something into the hedgerow that hems the drive.

Unable to see what it was, Roy turns around and walks back to the Station.

'Libby! He's comin' here.'

'Nah. He's probl'y callin' to the church. Looks like a preacher in that there high collar.'

'No. Look. He's already passed the church. But the hill's takin' its toll... such a shame... he set off so well an' all...'

'Strikes me a little unsteady on his feet, Miss Virna. Prob'ly a liquor salesman.'

'You know Jackson wouldn't send a liquor salesman up here.'

Libby leans forward to rub at the corner of a glass pane.

'Well, he's comin' here whoever he is. Looks kinda old though to be comin' up the hill in this heat.'

Between intakes of breath, Virna hears the slow, unsteady crunch of gravel as the man passes around the front of the house to the porch at the rear. The doorbell rings.

'Libby! Get the door. Hurry, girl.'

The furniture waits patiently as Libby patterns her way back into the hall. Virna hears the door being swung wide and a warm swath of minted summer air finds her where she sits behind the half shutter.

Libby returns carrying a small silver salver from the card-table in the hall. In her other hand is a gnarled walking stick that begins where the brown swirl of her fingers leaves off.

'Cain't say I remember folks still did this. Cain't say it ain't nothin' but a joke anyway!'

'What is it Libby? Bring it here to the light.'

Libby is visibly trembling.

'Cain't say you should trouble yourself…'

She drops the stick on the floor with a jarring clatter.

'Bring it here, girl.'

'No Ma'am, Miss Virna.'

'Bring it!'

'Yes Ma'am, Miss Virna.'

Virna plucks the card from the tray and turns it over onto her own hand. It drops into her lap as if it was iced and the merest touch of her skin had melted and slid it out of her grasp.

'Libby! What kind of a joke is this?'

'T'aint none what I'd call funny, Miss Virna.'

Virna studies the card, hoping for some mistake, but there it lay, edged in gold with a kind of wavy trim and small fancy holes punched in around the edges through which an enterprising young girl might thread a ribbon… a ribbon that she had shaken loose from her hair one early summer day… like the one outside…

'Send him away!'

'She can't do that, Virna, I just plain won't go.'

Virna turns her head slowly at the remembered richness of a man's voice, then quickly away again before she can see his face.

'And I say she can!'

Libby is standing behind Miss Virna's chair and staring fixedly out of the window as if she is afraid to look at the old man stooped by the doorway.

'If Miss Virna says I can, then mister, you better.'

'And who's going to pull you out the pond this time Libby? All shakin' wet an' mixin' with tears. An' who's going to lift you down from the orchard after Miss Virna done got you stuck up there again, chasing for moon-sized apples?'

Libby is shaking like she was still stood on that high wall, the tremor of her hands fluttering the black of the shawl as they hold to the chair.

'Don't you say those things. You hear me? Just don't you say 'em!'

Virna turns her face back to the window.

'You should listen to the girl, Richard. There's no cause for you to find us again at this end of our lives. It was better you hadn't come.'

'Do you know what a circle is Virna? It's a twist of rope that's full of beginnings because it has no end and so what else could it be made of?'

Virna sits, stony-faced, 'You broke our circle and you broke me and you broke this blasted hip and you took away my dancing shoes and my candles and music and nights without pain and summer grasses running wild under my feet and just... Go away.'

She closes her eyes, 'I wish you away. If all you can do after seventy years is talk in circles.'

The old man follows Libby's path through the drawing room. He catches her looking and smiles. She turns away from him back to the view outside the window.

'Life's a circle, Virna.'

'Have you looked in my mirror lately, Richard? This is what I look like at the end. An' I sure as hell don't need reminding.'

'This isn't the end, Virna. I'm here to show you how to begin.'

'A fine time, I'm sure. Libby! Get the door. The gentleman is leaving.'

'Nothing has to end, Virna. Look...' he holds a hand out into the air between them, '...there are so many beginnings if we just reach out and take them. They're like orchard apples on a fall day. They're everywhere you look. On the floor, in the air and hung around every which way in-between. You just pick the one that takes your fancy and bite right in! And if that don't work out or the worm beat you to it, you find a better one and try again.'

'And where was my beginning, Richard? Did I begin to dance again? Did I begin with gentlemen by the rack and my tray full of gilt-edged cards? Did I begin to forgive you for spookin' my buggy with that damned automobile?'

'Oh, you began alright, Virna. You began to suck in all that was sour and bitter and lost in the world. You began to close in on yourself and the people around you until we felt we were nothin' compared to your pain. You began to end. You bit that apple, worm an' all and you never threw anything away. It's all still there, stuffed like a cushion beneath you so you can sit there in your own shadow and brood about all the things that ended, just so you don't have to look up and see all these beginnings hanging in the air around you. Oh yes, you began alright.'

'If I ever began, Richard, it ended the day I sent you away.'

'And now I'm here to show you how to start again, Virna.'

'I'm sorry Richard, but my end is close upon me and your fine talk won't stop me or any of us from reaching it, one way or another.'

'Come with me, Virna. You too, Libby.'

'You cain't take Miss Virna nowhere! Just look at you, you cain't hardly stand let alone wheel this chair and I ain't been the length of that drive in years!'

'Trust me, Libby. Virna, will you come?'

'Can't say that I will, Richard. What Libby says is true, besides, this house is world enough for me and I don't trust outside. It's too sharp an' too wide.'

'Listen to me, Virna. Between us, Libby and myself, we can move the chair. Here Libby, help me turn it around.'

Libby is wild eyed and shaking. Her fingers are fluttering Virna's shawl until the whole room reeks of peppermint.

'C'mon girl, help me!'

'Libby. Don't you lift a finger!' Virna grasps the wheels of the chair firmly, 'And pray who's going to push me back up the hill when you two fools are plain wore out and fit for nothin'?'

'Trust me, Virna. You won't need to come back. This is a beginning, remember?'

'What foolishness is this, Richard?'

'It's not foolishness, Virna. It's a beginning.'

'And where will it end this time, Richard? In a fool's tears again?'

'That's up to you Virna, it's your beginning.'

'And you've come all this time back to ask me to be a fool?'

'They say there's no fool like an old one. So start by acting your age. Come on Libby, help push this damn chair.'

Libby folds the shawl over Miss Virna's hands and takes up one side of the handles. Between them they steer the chair along Libby's path through the drawing room and into the hall. As they pass the card table, Virna drops the calling card onto the bare wood.

'I may choose to consider it… later.'

Between them, Richard and Libby tilt the chair across the threshold until they are clear of the porch.

Virna turns around in the chair, 'Libby. The door.'

Richard pushes hard on the handle and the wheels begin to roll, 'Leave it, Libby. Doors are for opening, not shutting. This… is a beginning.'

The chair is hard to push on the gravel, but by the time they reach the front of the house Libby has stopped shaking and is beginning to put some weight behind her side of the handle. They pause for a moment at the top of the drive to watch it curve away towards the church.

Virna pulls the shawl around her, 'So much world.'

'So many moon-apples.'

She looks up as Richard speaks, then allows her gaze to follow the continuing sweep of the drive to where the Station sits with white clouds spewing out from under the gables.

'Well… I may as well begin by being a fool, I been most other things. Libby? Hold tight girl!'

The chair slowly gathers speed down the drive. Richard and Libby hold it from running away as Virna sits, stony-faced and rigid, half afraid.

'Hold on a minute.'

Richard digs in a heel and applies the brake. The chair halts not twenty yards from the house. Libby is panting.

'It's alright, Mr Richard. I'm okay. 'fact my head's never been this quiet for as long as I remember.'

As they set off again, she notices that Richard's stoop has gone. Twenty yards further and she sees Miss Virna's shawl becoming pale and grey, like the clock pigeons, and that Mr. Richard is standing straighter and his limp is now just a sometime stumble and that the air is warmer than it had been inside the house and that it still tasted like peppermint.

Virna's face is less lined now, but still immobile. The black fingerless lace gloves are now white and lay in her dark lap like a snowfall. By the time they near the church, Virna has her eyes closed and is showing the first faint trace of a smile.

'How are you at beginnings now, Virna?'

'Fine, Mr Clayburgh. Foolishly Fine!'

A few feet beyond the church, Virna asks them to stop.

'I think I might walk a step.'

'Then you'll be needing these.'

Richard pushes his hands into the hedgerow beside them and pulls out a handful of carmine satin and ribbon.

'My shoes! My dancin' shoes! Mr Clayburgh, for a gentleman you sure have a seductive way about you.'

'So you've begun to notice.'

Virna smiles openly at him.

'Libby! Help me put them on!'

Libby kneels down to take off Miss Virna's slippers before realising what she has done. She signs a cross over her breast, and admires the supple softness of her own knees as she laces and ties the ribbons. As Virna stands up from the chair the darkness slips from her clothes, leaving her bright and cautiously uncertain in the sunlight. She takes a step, wary at first, then one more. Suddenly, she skips. She stops herself and turns to laugh at Richard, but the old man is gone. The young man who stands there smiles down at her.

'Don't stop now, Virna. You've only just begun.'

'Begun what, Richard?'

'It doesn't matter Virna, it's just a beginning.' He jumps up, arms outstretched, 'Look, there's another! And there! Catch them on a breeze! Take them on the wing! They're yours.'

He links his arm through hers, 'Come on, we're late.'

Libby tags on behind, collecting summer flowers that pale against the print of her frock as Richard hurries them down to the Station.

Roy Jackson is waiting by the platform.

'Hi, Miss Virna, Mr. Clayburgh.'

Libby hangs behind Virna and Richard, a flush taking her cheeks. She can't remember Roy ever being quite so handsome.

'Hello, Roy.'

'Why, hello Miss Libby. I can't tell you what a pleasure this is. And on such a fine day!'

Beside them the engine seethes in the heat of the afternoon. Steam escapes the pressure dome on top of the boiler and blasts upwards, swirling into the shade of the gable roof from where it appears again, swelling out like young clouds percolating through the gingerbread fascias.

Virna pays the engine no more than a cursory glance, 'I thought it was afire!'

Richard steers her away towards the first carriage.

'We're almost ready now, Roy.'

'Sure thing, Mr Richard.'

Roy steps up to the footplate, then stops to admire a show of long slender legs.

'See you later, Miss Libby?'

'You may be sure that I shall give it great consideration, Mr Jackson.'

Richard hands Libby up onto the train. He turns to Virna, 'Almost forgot. I brought you this.'

From the inside pocket of his coat he offers her something slim and cellophaned with a golden ribbon around one end. Virna snatches it from him with glee.

'Why, Mr Clayburgh. Red-stripe candy. My very favourite.'

Richard lifts her into the carriage before staring back along the track. The engine that will take them onwards is as black as the absence of all light, but the blaze from the open firebox lights the mist of steam and the underside of the faded roof with a hopeful glow.

'Mr Jackson?'

Roy's hand lifts from the cab in reply.

Richard acknowledges it with an uncertain nod.

'I think we are ready.'

Hemmings wanders up the little side track by the church to find the old wheelchair unaccountably discarded in the drive. Without thinking too hard, he pushes it up towards the house. At the porch he finds the door swinging wide with the house empty and full of it's own echoes as usual.

Nothing seems to have been disturbed, and nothing seems to be missing... in fact, nothing much else, except a strong scent of peppermint.

He steers the chair through to the lounge and sets it behind the half-opened shutter, beside Libby's old, grey-dusty, high-back carver chair, where it always was. From a lingering sense of loyalty he corrects the old clock in the hall, then locks the door behind him to sit out on the bottom step.

His eyes close and his ears listen to the day filtering the trees, the pipe soon warm in his hand. He pushes his heels out into the gravel of the drive, leans his back against the porch column and waits for his son to return, but Vietnam is nigh forty years gone now... he shrugs and tamps the pipe with his tobacco knife... and it's not wise to fill your house with too many ghosts.

We are Golden

...was born from a belief in the connectedness of all living things down at some deep and probably as yet to be uncovered layer of existence. I searched for this connection and found a readily apparent one. Salt.

Once, when I underwent a process of self-examination, I discovered that I reacted to various situations in what I thought was a sophisticated manner that shaped and defined who and what I am, but I later found this to be a gross error.

What actually shapes and defines me is that I am an animal, and as such I am no better than any other animal that ever existed or will exist long after my demise. I am only different by design, and that is the sole distinction. You might say that we reason, and that makes us somehow better. Take a good long look at the world around you before you repeat that statement in public.

But those things that we describe sometimes disparagingly as animals are at least honest. A thing that as humans we intrinsically are not. If we were, we would never need the word 'apology'. In this story I see us as an extension of an animal kingdom spread wide across the globe and connected physically and neurologically by the salt in our tissues and in our breath and in our blood and in our shared future history.

The language is unashamedly philosophical and poetic in structure and I ask for the suspension of your disbelief in order to portray a world that I would wish to see.

If you don't enjoy it, then I apologise... but that only makes me human...

We are Golden

A man sits by the edge of a dune, digging his boots into the sand and trying for one last time to feel a part of the earth, but finding his soul has already slipped away. He lies back, relaxing, allowing the night wind to tousle his hair. The air around him condenses cold and pale upon his silver suit. The night itself is quiet, except for a wind keening sand across the margin, rustling the drying kelp and beneath all of that the indecent lap of waves careless upon the shingle.

He fastens the neck seal of the suit and leans forward into a sleeping wakefulness through which the waiting night pokes and prods him with its almost-silences. Giving up all fear of tomorrow, he rises to his feet.

Within a hundred steps he arrives once more at the place where the whale lies dark and fathomless across the strand. He sits down in its lee to clear his head and think. A swell rushes salt water into the shallow moat that has formed around it, washing the sand from its silver belly. Without fear, he leans against its night-black hide and uncorks the bottle from his pocket. He puts it down beside him in the sand and listens again to the wind. From deep inside the whale comes a dark, hollow, subcutaneous rumbling, as the gentle supporting hand of the sea drains away, leaving it to fall into ruin.

From its blow-hole issues a fine pink mist as the ruptured lungs fight to lift and lift again. A trail of red foam chases the drying starlight down the whale's flank to drip from the edge of a fin into the bottle. In the darkness, the man raises it to his lips.

He closes his eyes to dip momentarily into sleep.

Seconds later he is awake, his mind is shrieking, his baleen dry and empty of krill, his whole body wracked by pain and his lungs incandescent with agony.

He screams into the night and hears it rattle and fray amongst the shingle until it is lost.

As the scream subsides he feels the first touch.

The touch is cold at first, then spreads like liquid fire until it occupies his whole mind as one deep, cavernous thought. The man feels his own thoughts echo and skitter like forgotten, fallen leaves. He scurries them fearfully into a corner and waits.

A voice explodes within him, seeking him until there is nowhere to hide.

'So... *you* are Man.'

The voice falls silent for a moment, though the pain that surrounds it remains.

'I feel your mind within my own,' it says, 'Why do you bring so much pain?'

The man gathers his thoughts around him like a shield. From deep within them he waits for the sun to rise, for the pain-wracked nightmare to end.

Within the whale beside him a section of lung groans into ruin.

The man screams.

'So *much* pain,' says the voice, 'Why must you dwell upon it?'

Slowly, the man absorbs his own disbelief and learns to push aside the pain.

'Because I am a man,' he says, 'Pain is the fire that makes us what we are. In the absence of it we are never sure that we are alive. But what are you?'

The voice is softer now, 'I do not have the words.'

'Then show me,' says the man.

There is a gathering in his mind, as if the voice is remembering a thing of great pride.

'I am…'

…and swelling the black cavern of their minds comes a sense of rushing darkness, cloaking their skins with an intimate, turbulent caress. They plunge deep, deep and deeper still, until their whole being is crushed beneath uncountable fathoms. The change comes. Their thoughts seek the brilliance of a single point of light far, far above. Now they rush towards it, barrelling upwards through bright phosphorescence, breaking out into warm airs before falling …and falling …and failing to reach another star.

The man finds himself shaking. His mind is filled with an aftershock of pride, frustration and fear.

The voice returns.

'What are *you*?' it says.

'I am…' says the man, 'No …wait. I will not show you the things we have been. There is enough pain between us.'

'Then show me what you will become.'

…and the man fills their minds with the image of a mighty tower. It strikes free, pencilling tomorrow's sky like a silver-bellied whale. Its motors press down against the air, press down against the sea, then lift it with a gentler hand, up to the place where stars are strewn like grains of salt...

'Why do you seek the stars?' asks the voice.

The man plucks at a loose string of thought.

'We are stardust.' He smiles, half-remembering an old song, '...and we've spent our souls trying to get back to the Garden.'

'When you were cast out,' says the voice, '...you took our star-salt with you.'

'That's such a long time ago,' says the man, 'I can't remember.'

'*We* remember,' says the voice, ...and the man is aware of the sea that surrounds them. Not just as water with it's labyrinthine, Leviathan depths ...but as a fluid link through every living thing it holds immersed in its cooling stream ...and every living thing in that stream remembering ...their memories flooding the globe ...diverted here by a sunken range, enhanced there by winds and perpetuated by the warm gulf, cold ice flows.

'Does nothing ever die?' says the man.

'There are many ways to die,' says the voice, 'But the sea remembers everything. Watch...'

And in the stillness of their mind's eye the man sees himself ...stumped, stunted and shapeless... pushed out of the sea by a desire for the stars, falling in myriad numbers before learning to stand and each one carrying the sea in his blood and finding that he is barely closer to the sky than he has ever been ...and yet still they climb, each upon the other until now they are on the brink ...and still the salt sea is in their taste.

'Dear God,' says the man, 'How dry we must seem to you ...and how alone.'

The voice is quieter now, quizzical and hesitant.

'Show me that which you would call God.'

The man opens his mind to let the vastness of the concept flood through into the space they share …and finds nothing more than a small, unqualified belief.

'There is so little,' he says, '…and yet to some …it means so much.'

He falls into silent contemplation of an uncomfortable, unverifiable fact.

The voice waits patiently, allowing the man to reach the surface along with his thoughts.

'Perhaps Gods are the vastness of all things,' says the man, '…perhaps we are wrought in their image but cast free to become whatever we may.'

And in the sharing of their mind's eye he stands naked, arms spread and spanning space into infinity.

The whale beside him shudders in internal displacement.

'Then perhaps you have many rooms in which to house these many Gods,' says the voice, '…perhaps as many as there are men.'

'There are but many beliefs,' says the man, 'That is *my* belief.'

He speaks into the night's darkness where it clings to him, cloaking the bright reflective surface of the pressure suit.

'And what is your belief?'

The voice returns, immeasurably multiplied, rushing in concert from the furthermost places of the visitable sea.

'We believe in the stars.'

'We too believe in the stars,' says the man, 'Tomorrow we reach out for them.'

'What do you hope to do with them?'

'We hope to take them for ourselves unto eternity.'

'Then you must be as Gods,' says the voice, '…to walk amongst the stars.'

'Perhaps we are,' says the man, '...but dry, lonely Gods.'

'When we pushed you out,' says the voice, '...we knew what you must one day become, though we did not understand there would be such isolation. We knew that one day you would stand high enough above us to reach out and take the stars but we never thought of the pain that would be its foundation. In our passion we have failed you. And in return, Man will give us our ultimate triumph. The stars.'

'It is *we* who seek the stars,' says the man.

'You are right,' says the voice, 'It is *we* who seek the stars. It is time you came back to the Garden.'

And the whale's mind shakes him and submerges him in the all-embracing sea as wave after wave casts him upon the shore ...and each time the shore shapes and changes him, encapsulating salts and the essence of the waters in the rich warm blood coursing through his body. He watches it defeat the harsh dryness of the Land. Feels it shake a moist wind into his lungs.

The man looks down to the tower of dawn flame beneath him. Its roaring heat searches the surface of the sea and on down through coral, kelp and reef into the past that had pushed him from its womb to stand here alone ...with less than a handful of salt with which to remember.

His hands reach out to pluck the stars that twinkle bright and hard around him.

'In all our lives,' he says, 'In all our search for the promise of what we may become, we never thought to look beneath us.'

He smiles then, as he remembers the words of the dying whale.

'Then you must be as Gods,' it had said.

Blood Moon

Set on the Greek island of Zakynthos, there is a paradox hidden within this story, but if Bram Stoker can get away with it, then I hope to slip in unnoticed under his cloak.

Blood Moon is about those holiday destinations that young single people are sold at the Travel Agents only to find that when they arrive, there aren't enough significant single members of the opposite sex to go around.

In those situations, it is amazing what opportunities may present themselves, no matter how loud the alarm bell rings, and what may seem unacceptable at home suddenly becomes intriguing.

There is sexism in here, and ageism, but I hope that I have portrayed them from a sympathetic and victimless perspective where they are experienced in their reversed roles.

There is eroticism in here too. Sensitive, lyrical and without an overt brashness, it appears more cerebral than physical, where the desire seems stronger than the act, and perhaps the more explicit because of that.

It begs several questions: What is fame? What is age if it becomes a flexible thing? Is sex a pleasure, or a weapon? Or is it a pleasurably adaptable weapon. And it returns to the animal question: Is survival as a species just another form of behavioural honesty?

Blood Moon

They run like this for quarter of a mile. Tom twenty feet or so behind her, watching the sinews turn and twist in her ankles, striking a line from the inside of her calf around the back of the knee and along the inner thigh where her tiny swim-suit wraps its pink Lycra against tight little buttocks.

Her legs are long and smooth. Her toes leave small deep swirls in the hard sand as she runs up onto the balls of her feet. He paces her along the water's edge, occasionally dipping his feet in and out of the surf, feeling it splash cold against his legs while she avoids it entirely.

She steps up the pace whenever he comes close. He wonders how she knows this, then hears the sound of his own feet clipping the water. He drifts sideways onto the silence of the hard-packed sand. The soles of her feet flash white at him, strobe-like, adding to the hypnotic fascination that has dragged him from his towel to follow her down the beach.

To his left the sea crashes and sucks gently, the sound pushed almost beyond his awareness by the erotic ease of her movement. Without warning, she slows. Tom steps up a gear to pace alongside her. She turns her face and he stumbles in shock.

'Hi!' she says.

Her breath is clean and unhurried between beautiful teeth. She smiles and they flash quickly as the soles of her feet. Her eyes crease against the sun.

'It's OK,' she says, against the look on his face, 'You aren't the first.'

'I'm..?' Tom eases back on his stride to stay alongside her as she slows to a standstill, '…not the first …what?'

'The first to do a double-take,' she says, 'Like the one you just did.'

Tom draws a deep breath and leans forwards, fingers wrapping his knees. He shudders the breath back out.

'I thought for a moment …I knew you.'

'Liar…'

She spins on one heel to set off back along the beach. Tom sets off after her, his feet short-cutting the curve and slapping hard against the slow foam of the waves.

'Hey!'

She keeps on running. Tom notices he's falling behind.

'Hey!'

He steps up another gear, finds himself chasing her, mesmerised again by the sudden white flash of her feet. Soon he is pacing her, twenty feet behind and almost too tired to use his last breath in a shout.

'Hey!'

She stops abruptly mid-stride and hangs her head. Her features slide around in the shade, light playing across them as she turns to face him. The sun picks out the lines of sweat from her hairline, the way it turns to run along the wrinkles and creases around her mouth, her eyes, where crows feet tug life into the corners of a smile that might have sat more easily in a darkened bar.

Tom imagines a pale glass held between her sun-coppered, bony fingers, reflecting in the tan of her skin the small inconsistencies and changes wrought by time.

He pants in the heat, his arms swinging pale and white beside hers.

'Hey...' he says, his breath the only wind now they've stopped.

She stares back at him, calm and even-faced.

'Hey yourself.'

She lifts her face into the sun and as the skin stretches tight across her throat it transforms her.

'Once...' she says.

'Once?'

'Once... you might not have stumbled, or maybe for some other reason. Maybe I would've stopped you dead in your tracks.'

'And now?'

'And now you're looking at me. And now you stumbled back there at the top of the beach. And now you've shouted Hey! ...because you didn't believe what you saw ...and from the way you're looking at me you still don't.'

'That's unfair.'

'What's 'fair' got to do with anything?'

She turns and walks away. Tom watches her slender heel dip into the sand, the length of her foot roll up onto the surface where her toes dig back in to power her away along the beach, the first tension in her calves, her step beginning to lift like the hull of a speedboat rising from the water.

'Hey!' he says.

She stops as she is about to run, heels sinking back into the sand. Tom follows the wake-marks in her footsteps where she'd begun to lift away from him. He covers them with his own as he catches up to her.

'Like all young men,' she says without turning, 'Such a limited vocabulary.'

Tom turns his face away from her, feeling the sun burn into the back of his neck. He scans their path along the beach. His friends are nowhere in sight and, despite their company, for Tom this had been something of a solitary holiday. The island is a strange place, a blend of couples and ages that had left him feeling isolated and uncomfortable.

He digs his toes into the cooler sand just beneath the surface.

'I just... wanted to know.'

'How old I am?'

'No... no. I mean, how do you stay so fit?'

'For my age?'

Anger brings a sudden heat to Tom's face.

'What do you want me to do? Pity you? Because you've lived a bit?'

She smiles, and the sun-flash of those beautiful even teeth diffuse the anger from his face.

'Guess it's my turn to be sorry,' she says.

She jogs a short distance away across the beach. Tom looks around for where he's left his towel, realising she's led him right back there. He sits down to stretch the cramp out of his legs.

She stops and turns.

'Hey!'

'Hey what?' says Tom.

'Digging... and racing young men along the beach.'

'You always win?'

'Yep.'

Tom finds her again on the third day of not looking. He's convinced himself that he'll just keep an eye out as he and his friends cruise the bars in the black heat of late evening, but finds himself searching for her in the Tavernas and restaurants and the floodlit pools they pass. On the third day he decides to vary his time on the beach. The early sun might tan him better, he suggests, it being much less fierce at that time of day. Des and Gerry thought he'd already had enough.

He is about to unroll his towel when he sees a slender figure digging the sand close to the edge of the surf. As the figure leans over the spade he recognises the shape of the legs. He slides his trainers under the towel and pads out towards the edge of the sea.

'Hey!' she says, without turning. She pushes one hand through between her knees and wriggles her fingers in a wave.

'Hey yourself,' Tom says, 'How'd you know it was me?'

'I didn't.'

She lifts her hand from the beach to drop a coiled sand worm into the small bucket by her feet.

'For the fish.'

'You keep fish?'

'Nope.'

'Okay...' says Tom.

'For the ones we're going to catch.'

'Okay...'

She stands up to grin at him.

'The ones we're going to eat.'

'Hey...' says Tom.

'Back to Hey already. Like I said, such a limited vocabulary.'

'Now, hold on...' says Tom.

She slides the handle of the bucket into his hand.

'No, you hold on… to this,' she says, 'And don't stretch your vocabulary. You don't need to around me.'

Tom looks around to see if they're being watched but the sky is a blue unmarred by bird or cloud and the beach still mercifully free of towels, except for his.

Wherever she's moved she has left behind a small hole in the sand. The moist grains are steadily falling in as if timing turtle eggs, buried a mere hand-span beneath the golden reflective layer.

'I didn't come here to be insulted,' he says.

His voice carries with it a sense of smile. She looks up to see if she's heard it properly and drops the spade so her hands can fall one each side of his broad muscular hips. She looks him up and down, nodding once in approval.

'What's your name?'

Tom looks beyond her. They are still alone.

'Tom. What's yours?'

'Helena.'

'Nice. What about the fish?'

'I don't know the name of the fish.'

Her face is folding into mischief, the fading lips clipping the brilliant edge of her smile.

'Feel like a run, Tom?'

'Okay.'

'That's my boy.'

She hoists the spade and takes off like a rocket along the beach.

No matter how hard Tom pushes, she always manages to stay at least four paces in front. He runs for what seems an age of tortured breath, clinging hard to the bucket and pumping out last night's alcohol and second-hand cigarette smoke until they round the headland at the end of the beach.

In the next cove, much to Tom's delight, there are several small shanties made from driftwood and tin sheets, some with TV aerials sticking crazily up on long poles sunk deep into the sand. He follows her footsteps to a nearby shack that nestles where an outcrop of stone has crashed like a wild winter moment of sea.

The shanty is above the ground, perched high on long poles. The floor above his head is a lattice of bamboo and salvage plywood. A short wooden ladder leads up to an old house door laid flat. She pushes this open and helps Tom up into the shade of the tin and brushwood ceiling. He lays there catching his breath, his heaving chest tiger-dappled by the sun prowling the gaps in the roof.

'Home,' she says.

Across one wall an old couch covered by a tartan throw looks as if it has been recently occupied. Opposite that, an odd arrangement of iron plates shackle together into a semblance of a stove. Pans hang on wires fixed through the trellis walls. A collection of fishing poles lean in a corner. Beneath a blinded window sits a stash of towels, all different colours and textures, the floor around them lightly scattered with sand from their feet. An open shelf gathers a pile of knickers mixed with swimsuits between two or three worn paperbacks. A small half-cup bra swings suggestively from a hook on the wall.

'Home?' says Tom.

'Most of the time,' she smiles, 'Do you fish?'

'No.'

'Want to learn?'

'Okay.'

She hands him a pole with a coiled line attached.

'Where's the bucket?'

'Outside by the ladder.'

'Good,' she says, 'I thought you'd dropped it.'

'I'd have caught you if I hadn't been carrying that bucket.'

She laughs out loud at that, a spark of smooth, light-flowing sound inside the shiver of shade cast by the incompleteness of the shelter.

'Why'd you think I gave it you to carry?' she says.

In the centre of the cove, between her shanty and the others, a small river bursts a way across the beach to be swallowed by the sea. They stand at the edge of the ankle-deep fresh water while she baits their hooks.

'Hold the pole in one hand...'

She takes hers in her right hand, gripping it about two feet up from the bottom.

'...and twitch the end, like you were trying to shake something off it.'

Tom grips the pole and twitches it violently. The hook and bait snake out and jerk back in an arc ending at his feet. He reaches down.

'Don't pick it up,' she says, 'Unless you know what you're doing. I've seen people catch their own thumb before they know it ...and I don't want you with sore hands.'

Tom twitches the pole again, gently this time, and the bait flies out to where the outflow of river blends the incoming waves into a flat irregular pool.

'That's right.'

She twitches her own pole until it bends back in a practised arc, then flicks the baited hook right out to the end of the line.

'You've done this before,' says Tom.

'Once or twice.'

'Why here?'

'It's where the fish like to be. The fresh water brings insect larvae and things that people throw in. Things the fish don't normally get to eat. They swim around just out there where the water turns salt enough for them. They dip in and out of the fresh water but they never swim up here. So we have to go get them where they are.'

'No,' says Tom, 'You, I mean. Why here?'

'It's as good a place as any, and better stocked than most.'

'Have you been here long?'

'As long as I've been anywhere.'

She crinkles her eyes against the sunlight climbing high over the water, its fire sparking the wave tips.

'No-one snoops here, and no-one cares or comes to see what you're doing as long as it doesn't affect them.'

Tom presses the heel of the rod into the sand and sits down.

'What if you're in trouble?'

She does the same with her rod and sits beside him.

'Then, I guess, you're in trouble.'

'Say for instance… if I was to take you back into the hut… and try to make you see things… my way.'

She sits, staring silently into his eyes. Tom feels the tension lift between them and for a moment he wants to push it and see which way it will go. To see if it will rise up and surf along the sand like herself, running, or if it would lightning-flash back at him like the soles of her feet.

'Then no-one would come,' she says, '…and I'd be in trouble.'

He hides his expression from her then, knowing that the look on his face might push her away. For the first time since they'd met he felt he'd surpassed her and now she was running behind him, watching the soles of his feet lickety-splitting across the beach. The balance of power shifts between them in the silence like surf across the racing sand, until she says...

'And so would you.'

After an hour she has six fish and Tom has none.

'What are they?' Tom asks, as she splits and guts them on the iron plate of the dead stove.

'Sardines. Hardly enough for dinner ...but I have some tomatoes and other bits and pieces left over. We'll do fine.'

'I can't stay,' says Tom. 'They'll be looking for me. You've seen the headline before. Englishman missing on holiday, towel and trainers found on beach.'

Her face illuminates with laughter at his false concern. The folds of skin softly smooth away as the light in her eye settles down to a warm sardonic glow.

'You think anyone would care? You're English. They're just glad of your money then glad to see you go.'

'My friends will wonder.'

'The ones in the bar last night in town? The ones who tried to pull that moronic gaggle of shrieking young women while you didn't?'

'You were there?'

'While you sat there with this big question mark of a face? While you ignored them all and went home early?'

'Where were you?' says Tom, 'I...' His face lowers in the shade and he feels the quick heat rise again, 'I... I looked for you.'

'I know you did,' she says, 'But I wasn't ready to be found. Help me light the fire. They won't be looking for you yet. The matches are under the stove.'

They eat sardines straight off the stove plate with their fingers. Tom finds bread keeping cool in a bag under the couch. She sprinkles salt in the remaining juices, tears the bread into flat-sided chunks and presses it with her fingers onto the hotplate until it is soaked and salt-browned on one side. Tom eats until he feels stuffed.

She pulls the cover from the couch and folds it roughly behind him. She puts a hand on his shoulder and pushes him gently down onto it.

'Wait there.'

She lifts the door in the floor and climbs swiftly down the ladder. Tom closes his eyes and listens until the sand from her feet rasps again on the bottom rung. She climbs into the shelter and lays the door closed. In her hand is a bottle of local wine.

'I bury it in the stream.'

She passes the bottle to Tom. It is ice cool, and welcome compared to the heat in the room. She throws him an opener from a wire hook on the wall.

'Glasses?' he says.

'One mug. We'll share it from the bottle. Unless you're afraid you might catch something?'

Tom rubs his hand over his full stomach.

'Couldn't catch anything today.'

'You're carrying the worms again.'

'No,' says Tom, 'Only the fish.'

'And inside the fish?'

'Oh, Jesus.'

'Right this minute they're wriggling around inside you looking for the way out.'

Tom laughs, 'Stop it.'

'Then I think we'd better drown them in some wine, don't you?'

He stops laughing long enough to look her in the eye.

'Doesn't it worry you? That no-one knows I'm here? That I could do... anything?'

She stares at him, a curious expression on her face, half-mocking, half-serious. She tips her head downwards, the movement itself almost an act of submission. Her eyes fall into shade where he can't read them, turning their sockets into dark and deep recesses in her skin where the folds and lines lie hidden, waiting for an appropriate expression to make it's way to the surface.

She lifts her eyes back to his and holds him, steady and fearless.

'Should it?'

'You never know.'

Beside his man's body she seems inordinately small and slender, twig-like and ultimately vulnerable. They sit together, their legs pointing in opposite ways like the hands of a clock. The straps of her costume shrink away from the bones of her shoulders and deep hollows form where the musculature of her arms and neck meet, the fine tone of her body showing the bones open and apart.

Tom touches her gently with the tip of his finger, tracing it around the hollow before lifting the edge of the material with his nail and sliding his finger into the space between lycra and skin. He moves it gently backwards and forwards.

'I went to kiss the feet of the Saint,' she says.

She closes her eyes and sways slightly until the soft downy hairs of her arm mingle with the darker, coarser ones of his.

'They bring him out of the church once a year and carry him around the town in an upright glass casket.'

Her weight shifts and she leans against him with an unexpected lightness of touch.

'There's a hole in the bottom where his foot peeks through. Once a year they give him a new pair of gold slippers. It's supposed to be good luck to kiss them. I went early. I can't get near them on Saint's Day.'

'Is he dead?'

She smiles to herself.

'Not for long. Four, maybe five hundred years.'

'Long enough.'

Tom passes her the opened wine bottle. She does no more than wet her lips before passing it back.

'He was buried on the hill above the town. When they dug him up thirty years later he was still perfect. As the procession passes, people throw themselves under the casket to be cured.'

'Does it work?'

'Sometimes, I guess.'

Tom slides two more fingers under the strap and lifts it clear of her shoulder to rest against her arm.

'When are you leaving?' she asks abruptly.

'Sorry,' says Tom, 'I shouldn't have done that.'

He lifts the strap back into place on her shoulder. She shrugs it off again and leans into him.

'No. I meant for home.'

'Oh. Next Sunday.'

'You'll be here then. For Saint's Day.'

She touches his hand with a finger.

'Next Saturday.'

Tom takes her shoulder in his hand, empowered by the way the small bones are completely hidden inside his palm and fingers.

'When they fire the stubble,' she says.

Tom moves his hand around, watching his skin pass possessively over hers. He slides it to her neck and notices the way his fingers fasten easily around it. She closes her eyes and a small impulsive swallow disturbs her throat, rippling downwards beneath his fingers. For a split second he squeezes. Her breath catches in her throat and she becomes still beneath his hand, except for the quickening pulse inside her. He relaxes his grip.

'Along the peninsula,' she says, '...the smoke turns the sunset into an inferno.'

He studies her face in silence.

She speaks again without opening her eyes.

'You should see the moon.'

'I've seen moons,' says Tom.

'Not like this.'

'Moons aren't special.'

'Moons become special. When you're old.'

'How can you tell?'

'Because I'm very, very old.'

Tom watches her face and the way she moves within her skin.

'Liar...'

With his thumb he stretches her throat until the lines disappear. His fingers spread across her face. Smoothing behind them, they push into her hairline until the skin flattens and shines with an inner glow. He watches the years of light slowly working their way outwards from where the sun has pushed it deep into her bones.

He recalls her every movement, flowing and constant as a trade wind as she ran the beach. Within the breadth of his fingers is the weight of every smile she ever made. Lifting her face to his, he contemplates her lips. They are full now, and slightly parted with anticipation. Behind them are perfect teeth... and something inside him clicks.

'I know you,' he says.

He lifts her face all the way to his, and kisses her smile.

She shudders a deep breath.

'No, you don't.'

'I do, I'm sure.'

'You only think you do.'

'It's more than that. I think you're famous.'

'No.'

'You are. I know it.'

'No. …look, maybe… maybe once.'

'No-one stops being famous,' says Tom, 'They go to Video Heaven and live forever on a little silver disc.'

'What if I don't want to live forever?'

Tom thinks for a moment.

'If I killed you now,' he says, '…you'd be even more famous.'

'I don't want to be famous,' she says.

'But you'd live again.'

Tom grips her shoulders tightly.

'They'd drag out the celluloid, turn back the clock and parade you all over the television.'

'For a week,' she says.

Tom laughs, relaxing his grip.

'A week's a long time in immortality these days.'

'It isn't,' she says, '…and the longer you live the harder it gets. You stack up all the things you've ever needed to do and come the morning the weight of that keeps you pinned to the bed.'

He laughs, 'You look like a woman who's been pinned to the bed.'

She kisses him quickly and lightly.

'I'll admit to once or twice,' she says, '…in a very long career.'

Tom stands and lifts her to her feet. She comes clear off the floor as if she contains no substance at all.

'No wonder you run so fast.'

She slips the strap off her other shoulder. Stepping out of the swimsuit she moves up against him. Her tan is complete.

Her body is tight and lithe as any woman a third of her age. Tom slips out of his shorts and his body rears against her, pressing hard into her tight belly. She stands on tiptoe to whisper something darkly indistinct in his ear.

Tom wakes on the couch with the sun streaming through the roof. The shack is empty and the last thing he remembers is holding her naked in the middle of the room. He grabs his shorts and climbs down the ladder to find her but the beach is entirely empty.

He waits a while then returns along the shore. His towel and trainers are still where he'd left them. Back at the apartment there is a note on the breakfast bar.

Moved into the Terrazza Hotel with Cheryl and Lesley. Don't wank yourself silly. See you at the airport a week on Sunday. Des and Gerry.

Tom spends the next two days pacing the beach, walking the bars alone at night and visiting the shanty in the cove. He waits for her outside, sitting in the flow of cool water from the river. He once, and only the once, opened the door from the ladder and looked in. It was as if he'd walked away just a moment ago, except that the half-cup bra was missing.

From the river-water he watches people from the other shanties further along the cove. They never look his way and he never seeks to attract them. As they walk past, their skin dark as honeyed toast, they ignore him totally.

On the third day, Tom is asleep on the beach under a book in the early sun. The pages lift from his face and sudden sunlight breaks open the lids of his eyes. He looks around and for a moment can see nothing but the glare of sand and the bright shatter of water across the beach, then in the midst of it all a pair of lean, tanned legs, hurrying away from him to run the water margin.

He lurches to his feet and stumbles off after them.

'Hey!'

She looks over her shoulder briefly and steps up a gear. Tom follows, staggering, his heart struggling to restore the bloodflow to his still-sleeping muscles. He eases back as he realises she is heading towards the cove. He slows to a steady jog as she powers away into the distance.

The cove is deserted when he arrives. The shanties further along look the same as before, aerials clawing wildly at the sky, wisps of pale smoke slanting from one steel chimney and the faint scent of frying sardines sharpening the still air.

Her shanty seems quiet and empty. Somewhere along the way he's lost her footsteps and the only recent ones lead away from the foot of her ladder. Tom retraces them and climbs, pushing open the trapdoor above his head.

Inside, sunlight wickers the shaded room, in a few places it sears, bar-like and solid. Tom walks slowly through as if it has substance. On the stove are desiccated sardine heads, scrapings of dry tomato skin and bread.

In the centre of the room he stops and turns around, arms outstretched, finger tips wide and sweat drying on the little webs of skin. He shucks off his swim shorts and stands naked, enjoying the sunlight striping his skin. There is a scent in the room, perhaps no more than his memory. He closes his eyes, touches himself, and his penis rears in his hand. He opens them again to find the edge of the door lifted and her eyes watching him.

Tom is amazed that she is not in the least embarrassed. She climbs up through the opening to stand beside him. He moves his hand forward and touches her, anywhere so long as he can feel her skin on his.

She takes his penis in the feather touch of one, long-fingered hand. She moves it slowly and Tom throws back his head to gasp. She reaches up and pulls his face down to hers, kissing him, her lips wide and searching, her tongue parting his teeth and forcing a way through his mouth. He wraps it with his and stands there trembling.

She places her hand under his chin and lifts. Slowly their mouths tear apart and his head is pushed back until he can see nothing but the roof of the hut and the light that pours through it and pulses his eyes. He sways while she manipulates his body in a way he had never dreamed possible.

Tom drops to his knees on the towel-covered floor. She unhooks the swimsuit straps from her shoulders and slowly sheds it, moving snakelike to ease it past her hips. The heat from her exposed skin falls in waves upon his. With eyes still closed he leans forwards to bury his lips into the soft skin of her belly. She places both hands behind his head to massage his neck and ears, running her fingers through the short hairs, and with one dark finger traces ley lines beneath his skin that only she knew existed.

Tom is kissing her belly, harder now, frantically grinding his tongue into her navel.

She leans down to whisper something in his ear and the tremors leave him. His muscles relax and his penis softens. He is at a place of perfect ease. He has no sense of after-shock. His penis is still dry and the ache of unspent seed is subsiding in his groin with no regret.

'Not yet,' she says.

She helps him to his feet.

'Come with me.'

She takes him by the hand to lead him willing and naked through the trapdoor and down the ladder. They walk to where the river cascades across the sand.

'Lie down,' she says.

Without hesitation Tom settles himself into the flow of crystal water. His back finds the sun-warmed sand below it's surface and relaxes.

She picks up a handful of fine sand to gently scrub the soles of his feet. Tom shuts down the contradictions of hot sun and cool water while the rest of his existence becomes centred on her touch. Taking each leg in turn, she scrubs away an old layer of sun-scorched skin from Tom's body. She sits astride him, lifting him, turning him, chasing every hidden fold and secret place of his body until Tom understands that no-one could know him better than this.

She helps him to his feet and his skin blazes with soft fire, his face shining out like a beacon. He has never been so alive. He takes her hands in his.

'My turn,' he says.

She lays down by the edge of the water and gives herself up to his hands. Tom is careful, as she had been, but the touch of his hands and the scent of cool water splashed across her skin alone are enough to bring her body swelling up to meet his fingertips.

He helps her to her feet and his body responds to her glowing nakedness. He crosses the stream in two strides to find himself on the other side of the river, towards the other shanties.

'Let's take a quick run up this side of the beach to dry off.'

He sets off a couple of steps, then realises she isn't following.

'I can't,' she says. She turns away from him to walk back to her side of the cove.

Tom runs back to catch her.

'What's the matter?'

'This is my side of the beach... I never go over there.'

'Is there someone over there you don't want to see? Is that it?'

'Something like that, I can't tell you why. Not yet. Maybe not ever.'

Tom finds himself inexplicably angry. He grips her hard by the shoulders until her feet leave the floor.

'I could make you.'

'You couldn't,' she says, 'Or if you could you might as well kill me now.'

'I don't want to make you that famous…'

Tom wonders why the words filter through his teeth the way a lie does.

'…I just want to make love to you.'

'Then come with me.'

She leads him by the hand back to the shanty where the only sounds are the mix of distant slow waves and the deeply uneven wrack of their own breath. A sharp pungency of dried sardines and tomatoes descends over the bright sharp cleave of their own fresh bodies.

Tom sinks to his knees and begins to kiss her. He searches with his thumbs until he opens the bright pinks and gentle scarlets he'd found by the side of the stream. He presses his face against them and the tip of his tongue reaches out to enter her.

To his surprise she is tight, almost virginal. He pushes harder until the warmth of her flesh grips the whole of his tongue. Her legs stiffen under his hands and his penis slips out from between his folded thighs.

She places a hand each side of his face and lifts him to his feet. She pushes his chin backwards with one hand until he stares once more at the roof before closing his eyes. Her perfect white teeth close around the crown of his penis. Her tongue is like nothing he could have imagined. He wants her... now.

His hands fill with her hair as he lifts her roughly to her feet. He drops her carelessly on the couch, covering her with his body, the fingers of his left hand reaching for an opening into her. She lifts her mouth to his ear and whispers two indistinct words. Tom sags against her like a corpse.

She slides out from beneath him to sit at his side, stroking his penis, and admiring the way his so-young body holds itself together as if it were freshly stitched into new skin. He is still hard, even while asleep like this, and while he sleeps she fills her mouth with him, squatting at his side with knees apart, her own sex open and protruding.

With a long bony finger she spreads the wet lips and slowly finds her own satisfaction.

She picks her swimsuit from the floor and leans down to kiss his eyes.

'Tomorrow,' she says.

When Tom awakes she is gone. While he waits for her return, the sun falls below the roof of the shanty to bleed fire through the walls. The air around him is latticed with sunset flame. He sits on the couch and closes his eyes again, trying to recapture why it was he thought he'd known her. Or perhaps that he's just dreamed that he knew her.

He walks back along the beach to the apartment for a shower.

Dressed for the evening in slacks and shirt, Tom makes his way back to the shanty. At the foot of the ladder he calls softly but there is no reply. He pushes open the trap door and climbs up into the darkened room. Stars shine here, feathering in and out of existence against the roof as he moves. He's made up his mind to wait for her, however long that takes. In the bag he carries there is bread, an imported wine, a small round local cheese and a quarter-kilo of thickly-sliced ham. He makes his way cautiously to where he knew the couch was. He leans against it... and touches warm skin. He recoils at once, falling back onto the bag.

'Hey,' he whispers.

There is no reply, only the ear-bursting sound of his own snatched breath and his heart in his throat.

'Hey.'

He reaches out to touch her arm. She makes no move but he feels the warmth of her flesh and the small, slow pulse in her wrist. He sits on the floor with his back to the couch. He clasps his arms around his knees and waits.

After a while, in which the moon broached the roof and replaced the stars, he tries to wake her again. She makes no sound at all. In the semi-darkness he runs his hand across her body. She is naked. He strokes her skin. In the dark she is flawless. He kisses her perfect nipple and it puckers erect as if his lips had been a winter's breath. He strokes around her eyes with a fingertip and finds no trace of lines. The crow's feet around her lips have fallen away to be replaced by soft, moonlit skin.

He touches her hair. It is soft and clean, seemingly untouched by the years of sun and salt winds with many more still to come. He closes his fingers around her arm and shakes her gently. There is no response. He shakes harder, but she lays there wrapped only by the darkness, entirely extinguished except for the slow, steady pulse in her wrist and the shallow butterfly of her breath.

Tom could never have explained the anger that surged through him. It came from somewhere animal deep inside, an old echo but at once instinctive and raw. He thought at first it was born of the way she controlled him ...dismissing his own needs and replacing them with her own …but no …it came from much further down than that.

The fingers of one hand close around her slender throat, relaxing only as he brings this instinct to kill under control once more. He lifts her from the couch by her shoulders to shake her awake, the blonde of her hair chipping the moonlight bars striking through the hut.

There is no response to his effort. Tom drops her back on the couch and fumbles around for the stove. He finds the metal leg and searches around it for where he'd seen her stash the matchbox. His hand closes around them. He pushes her into a sitting position and strikes a match. The winnowing light sheds shadows across her features as the match sways in his hand. He cups his eyes to shield them from the brightness of the flame so he can study her face. She is beautiful. With the light from the flame she seems on fire herself, her skin filled with a joy and serenity.

Her eyes open wide. The match burns his fingers before she blows it out. The darkness envelops him again, deeper than before, and this time with a bright orange ball inside his eyes beyond which he can't see. Her hand touches his face and Tom chokes on a half-drawn breath.

'Hey,' she says softly, 'I said tomorrow.'

'You don't you understand,' says Tom, 'I want you now.'

'No,' she says, 'Tomorrow.'

'No. Not tomorrow. I want you now. So much that it hurts. Make the pain go away.'

'No.'

Tom rips open his shirt. Sliding out of his slacks he stands naked in the darkness.

'Wait,' she says, 'Here. Let me touch you.'

In the darkness she takes him, manipulating him in slender fingers that make shapes only his mind can see. Her touch stands all of his consciousness along one vivid knife-edge. His instinctive senses retreat inwardly, afraid of the fire she is creating around the end of his penis.

'Stop that...'

He wrenches himself away. His hands find her shoulders in the darkness and he throws her back onto the couch. He falls across her and his knees force open her legs.

She screams in his ear.

'Tomorrow!'

'No,' says Tom, 'Right Now... or never.'

'But this isn't right! Not the way I wanted.'

She gasps under his weight, forcing his mouth away from hers.

'I have to see the moon!'

Tom braces himself above her, the face he'd seen by match flare as bright in the eye of his desire as if she'd been struck instead by moonlight.

'When I make love I have to see the moon,' she says, '...red with the smoke from the burning stubble. It has to be a bright, full, blood moon or I can't go all the way back ...and the fires aren't started until Saint's Day. Not until tomorrow.'

'What about what I want?'

'Tomorrow,' she says, 'There'll be a moon like you'll never see again.'

'No!' he says, 'Now!'

His hand thrusts between her legs, roughly parting the fragile opening of her body.

'And again tomorrow!'

'No ...wait.'

She relaxes under him, the defensive arch of her body gives way, accepting him.

'Not like that.'

She pushes his hand away and strokes his erection. She uses the wetness of the tip to gently moisten the edges of her hidden lips.

'Here... like this.'

She pulls him inside her, the constriction of her body breaking his skin as she forces him deep. She breathes two indistinct, arcane words ...and in one split second he begins to come. She pulls his lifted his head down to hers and moves her lips upon his mouth. He opens it wide and her tongue pushes inside. He sucks her into him, filling his mouth and throat with her dark fleshy heat until he feels the end harden and roll into a tube which forces it's way past his own tongue, pushing inwards, choking off his breath.

He tries to pull away but the arms wrapped around his head crush him ever tighter to her. Her tongue pushes deeper until it tears the fragile larynx, crushing brachia and aeoli, mixing the blood draining into his lungs with her own saliva before severing the path of a major artery. She drains him completely in the length of a single orgasm.

A silver moon passes slowly over the tin sheeting, rippling its pale silk through the walls and across their entwined bodies. She wakes and pushes Tom to the floor with an unnatural ease. She lifts the trapdoor to slide him down the ladder to the sand below. She picks up the spade and begins to dig.

Three feet down, a pile of white bones lift light out of the sand. She throws the shrivelled remains of Tom and his ripped clothes on top of them and shovels the sand back in, smoothing the surface with her feet.

She climbs back up the ladder ...and closes the trap.

As she runs the beach next morning a young man is waiting by the edge of the surf.

He steps into her path.

'Hey!' he says.

She slows and stops to answer him.

'Oh, sorry,' he says.

'For what?'

'I thought…'

'You thought I was younger, eh?'

'Well… no… a lot older, actually.'

'That's alright then.' She laughs brightly at his discomfort, 'I was once.'

He shakes off the absurdity of the comment.

'I'm looking for my friend. We haven't seen him for days and we fly back tomorrow. Someone said they'd seen him running along the beach after a blonde with long tanned legs… at first I thought… but they said she was much older than you.'

'I think I should be flattered.'

'Anyway… sorry to have bothered you.'

'No bother. Hey!' she says, her teeth flashing white inside the smile, 'Anybody ever tell you you're cute?'

'Only my mom.'

She laughs out loud and spreads her arms around him in a half-circle. Fine-toned muscles ripple inside her pink swimsuit.

'You're *Fit*,' he says.

She takes his hand in hers and spreads the fingers with her own. His skin is full and flushed with youth in the way that makes her despair, for far more centuries than she cares to remember it has been wasted on the young.

'But you know that,' he says, 'How do you..?'

'Stay that way?'

'Yeah.'

'Digging. And racing young men along the beach.'

A Day for Tigers

Please allow me this indulgence of writing something that I desperately wanted, nay, needed, to write.

I had been reading Sigmund Freud's psychodynamic theory on the composite human personality of Id, Ego and Superego, and the complex systems and internal struggles that this tripartite mental structure sets up within the average human being.

It is easy, when reading the attributes of each of these components, to quite logically see them as individuals, vying for supremacy or, as a best result, a kind of uneasy socialising balance. If you understand this concept, then I won't preach to the converted. For all others, there is Google.

I decided on the basis of what I had learned to take a critical look at one successful person, and to disseminate his life and thought processes in line with the Id, Ego and Superego as described by Freud.

Alexei Kalenikov, a Russian Cosmonaut, became my unwitting victim. He finds himself torn between his need for the assistance of the other two Cosmonaut companions, Ivaan and Boris, and the need to embrace and practice his own obsessive self-sufficiency.

I didn't know where this story was going when I began it, only that just beneath it's surface were forces that, once unleashed, can bring great success or great tragedy.

So come on out to the Asteroid Belt. There are tigers out there...

A Day for Tigers

In this, the smallest of houses, there are no gutters or pipes to swallow the rain. No sweet-scented bitumens and creosotes to line them. No father's feet upon the ladder that racks the window. No black gobs of seed-filled earth falling around me.

From inside this suit I sense the instability of its foundation. It moves with plates and rings and seals. Settles with unease. Pulsing with conduits and circuitry, it holds me naked except for my name, Alexei Kalenikov. And that too was once my father's. I look out of the window to see his feet.

The bright star of the Orbiter steals below the horizon.
And for once... the world is still.

Boris

'Ivaan?'

'I hear you, Boris.'

'Don't deploy the rear struts. They'll restrict your angle of ascent.'

'I think I'll have to.'

'There should be enough mass with you and Kalenikov inside to stop the Egg from rolling.'

'Alexei is outside.'

'What's he doing outside?'

'You ask him.'

'Kalenikov!'

Silence.

'Is he disconnected?'

'Wouldn't surprise me. Wait until the dust settles. I may be able to see him.'

'I have only five more minutes.'

'Should be enough… wait… I see him now.'

'What's he doing?'

'Scraping the dust from around the base of the boulder with his foot. There's red dye everywhere. Hold on.'

'What is it? Get it on screen.'

'There's dust on the camera. Can you make it out?'

'It's square. It's a square edge. He's dyeing it red. What is it?'

'Looks like a plinth. He's dyed two sides now and they're both square. Hold on. He's coming around the back.'

'Where is he? Get him on screen.'

'Hold on while I shift the camera.'

'I see him.'

Kalenikov. Out there in the dust making a square at the lens with your fingers. What are you doing? Why aren't you back in the Egg with Ivaan?

'Ivaan?'

'Here.'

'Squirt the bastard. Use the lance.'

'This is Alexei we're talking about?'

'Exactly. Half-second burst should do it. Get his attention.'

'OK.'

I watch the image shake as the pressure lance needles out from under the front of the Egg. Kalenikov jerks like a puppet and the dust flies from his suit to hang in the low G. I see him tread vacuum beyond the left of the screen, anger leading every step.

'click... the fuck are you playing at?'

'Ahh. Alexei! Welcome back.'

'Boris, you bastard. I might have known.'

'Alexei, my dear, it takes at least two pairs of hands to get this Metal Chicken home so be a good comrade and stay plugged in.'

'Who's in charge here?'

'You are, my friend. But keep the riff-raff amused. Let us know what is happening.'

'I'll tell you when you need to know.'

'All I need to know is that you'll tell me. And look after the Egg.'

'Kalenikov... Out.'

Prodigies...

The dust snows the screen into a grey swirl and I sit back to listen in to their conversation. Let them play...

'Ivaan.'

'Yes, Alexei?'

'Deploy the rear struts.'

'If you come back inside Boris says we'll have enough mass to hold her still.'

'Ivaan!'

'OK.'

'Ivaan. This is not just a boulder. It's round, and about three metres in diameter.'

'Meteorite?'

'That comes mounted on its own plinth?'

'Then what is it?'

'Let's find out. Extend the left rear strut another fifteen centimetres. That should bring the lance across the base.'

'OK.'

'Fire now. One second burst... then traverse right five degrees and fire again.'

Kalenikov treats him as if he were a backward child. And each time, something inside Ivaan becomes crushed. I see it in his face. He folds inwards like a piece of emotional origami. I'm tired of prodigies... and I'm the good shepherd and Kalenikov is brilliant, intuitive, and crass...

I climb gently from the couch to watch the stars. Brace myself on the docking ring. Head up into the blister... and stare.

I never tire of the colours. Reds, purples, blue-shifted whites that stamp the retina. And all jumbled. And all so far away they're beyond price.

'Tigers in the Night' Kalenikov calls them. But out here they're hard and brittle. They look as if they would shatter against each other if I held them in the palm of my hand.

Below my feet the asteroid tumbles slowly past. Thirty kilometres in diameter.

Imperturbably green by sunlight.

Smooth and un-crimped.

Black as Hades on Darkside.

Ivaan calls it 'Kalenikov's Ego'.

Hubble found it. The albedo brought us. Bright and green amongst the glitter and black of the asteroid belt like the jewel in a ring. And now we're here we find it's just a gas that seeps in and out of the rocks, reacting with the sunlight.

I settle down to watch the clock and listen to the patient tick of small motors as the telemetry array constantly seeks to re-align. But the stars... this is what I came for. And yet despite that, in this period of darkness and silence, I find my thoughts drifting lightly as frost-smoke back to the Academy. I close my eyes but the stars remain, and against them, I hear the voice of my Grandmother,

'There are more prodigies here...' she would inscrutably remark, '...than you could shake a stick at.'

And why I am there too sometimes escapes me. Until I look around and see the others for what they are. Blunt instruments mostly, although some of them are magnificent hammers capable of prodigious impact, yet whose lives seem perfectly fitted between parallel lines that will never reach the horizon... without me.

Yet some are different. And some are strange. And the strange ones frighten and excite me because I see the tail of their comet passing through the orbit of mine and the prospect of collision is at once inspiring and fearful.

Some have never adjusted, and gradually the class is thinning as these maladroits disappear without leave or goodbye.

We do not ask where they have gone.

It is by our continued presence that we judge ourselves.

I call out to Ivaan in the corridor and he rushes past with the briefest of smiles, hurrying I don't know where, but I will bet Kalenikov is tugging seductively on the line, drawing his web tighter around us all.

As ever, Alexei is last into the lecture room. Professor Mareniko scolds him with a look that he pointedly and visibly ignores.

'Professor?' I call.

'Yes, Boris?'

'Sir... I...we...' and I sweep the room with my hand, 'have heard perhaps a joke... perhaps even a myth...'

'Yes, Boris?'

'About... Tigers, Sir.'

'Tigers... Hmm,' he seems amused for a moment, '...and why, today of all days, Boris, should you ask about Tigers?'

I glance outside the window to where the bridge arcs the river, held up by virtue of the way the stones press constantly against each other and the ground; suspended by a whisker of geometry, like ourselves in here, anchored between each other and the stars, building our strengths into an arch that will take us out beyond the atmosphere to where imagination's tigers stalk the darkness.

'It's…' I begin, but my eye is drawn outside again as the sun flashes the contours of the open, lifting landscape into dark stripes. I shift my gaze instantly to Kalenikov. Beneath the close-cropped blonde hair his face is impassive, as immobile and solid as the stones that foot the bridge but I know that within him there are parts that are stressed incredibly, so that the whole can hang together.

'It's… such a day for Tigers.'

Mareniko follows my gaze and pauses for a moment, the glare from outside creating shifting mirrors on the small round spectacles that hover above the straight line of his nose. His thin lips draw back against his snow-burned skin, framed by the slender moustache and small goatee beard.

'Yes,' he says, 'I agree.'

He walks over to the window and I know he sees the same raising of landscape, the same shutter-clicks of light and shade that play around the river at this time of day. He and I are similar. Not the same. I have learned that much in my time here… but I feel a sympathetic resonance in his thoughts, in the economy of his movement, in the time he takes to assemble his ideas into patterns, time indiscernible to everyone else. Without turning he says, as if requesting an answer from the glass,

'Why are you here?'

'I have often wondered that myself,' I reply.

'No… not just you, Boris… all of you.'

There are shrugs and chuckles, snide looks… and none of these going unnoticed in the reflection before his eyes.

Someone, in an apologetic tone, makes a comment about learning. Mareniko dismisses it without turning,

'Ivaan?'

Ivaan stammers when immediately confronted. He too needs time to assemble his thoughts, but once assembled he opens like the mnemonic flower he truly is.

'If... if... I may quote...'

'No, Ivaan. You may not.'

'Then...'

'Then one day, Ivaan... you may have an opinion of your own.'

Mareniko turns from the window, 'Kalenikov?'

There is no hesitation. Kalenikov fires the statement into the air for us all to see.

'Because I deserve to be.'

Mareniko nods, 'But how do you know this?'

'Because I am here.'

Mareniko turns and smiles; a canvas smile, paint cracking at the edges, aged and worn.

'So am I. And so is the cleaner who polishes the floor of your room every Tuesday...'

'Wednesday,' says Ivaan.

'...so what does it prove?'

'That I am the best.'

In Kalenikov's voice there is no sense of doubt. I wonder if he has ever been shamed in the way that makes the rest of us hesitant. I don't think he has. I close down the thought. Mareniko continues.

'How has this... hypothesis... of your worth been tested?'

'I know.'

'Then I feel you have an advantage over the rest of us, Kalenikov. Has anyone else here ever felt this degree of certainty? That Fate made them so?'

Smiles pass around the room as quickly as counterfeit notes, resting only upon the foolish. And I know that there are still fools amongst us.

'Boris?'

I jerk at the question in his tone. I feel resentment in the way he uses given names, especially myself and Ivaan. It is most belittling in its own way. Mareniko somehow enables Kalenikov by using his family name as an imperative. I recognize the way it works against us. We sit pyramidic, with Kalenikov at the apex. From the shadow of the bottom left-hand corner, I reply.

'I am only certain of one thing… that I am uncertain of everything.'

Mareniko returns to the window. I feel him pushing away in his thoughts the uncertain depth of snow that lays outside obliterating spring pathways and keeping warm the quietly reverberating bulbs and corms beneath the hidden verges.

'Good reply.'

A lorry makes its way slowly over the bridge, tyre tracks dark and parallel in the white. It pulls up a few metres away and men in winter camouflage leap from the canvassed back to stand shaking their limbs and stamping their feet. Bags are thrown carelessly by some unseen hand from inside the vehicle. The men pick them up and stomp off to the heat-lock doors of the nearby corridor.

Mareniko's gaze returns to a place half a metre in front of his shoe toes.

'I myself have heard a rumour. Has anyone else heard a rumour recently?'

He lifts his head to observe us. There are heads nodding around the room, especially from the ones whom I know share the cigarette ration of various soldiers that frequent the bar. The cigarettes we are forbidden to smoke. I heard the rumours from my mother. That gave me several versions from which to compose the most likely truth… that Kalenikov had returned from his 'pilgrimage' as he called it, with a hugely swollen ankle... and reeking of cat.

When he resumed classes he became more impassive and impenetrable than before; as now he sits. Since he uttered his last statement he has been immobile. I cannot even discern his breath... and I wonder if he even needs it.

Mareniko studies the floor half a pace away.

'And what do we know about the certainty of rumours? Kalenikov?'

'Sir?'

'Do you have an opinion on rumours?'

'Everyone has an opinion, Sir.'

'On rumours?'

'Not necessarily.'

'But an opinion nonetheless?'

'Yes, Sir.'

'And your opinion, Kalenikov, is...?'

'My own, Sir.'

Mareniko returns to his desk and shuffles his books into the place they occupy in his mind. I have seen him do this many times now... the order... the pedantry of place and access that I see in my own workshop... his protection against our defeat.

I look across to Kalenikov and see his profile against the light outside. His eyes have closed and yet he sits erect as always. There are no roads to understanding tracking his features, no traffic of thought flickering along a high cheekbone.

For how long I watch him I am unsure. In my peripheral vision Mareniko seems almost an automaton, shuffling and pressing papers in predestined patterns against the dark maroon of the desktop. I am aware that he has raised his glance towards me but inexplicably I cannot tear myself away from Kalenikov's closed eyes. A part of me hears Mareniko clear his throat and say,

'It seems we were wrong, Boris. Maybe this is not such a day for tigers.'

And I cannot answer him, for I am consumed by the sight of Kalenikov. I don't know why I am looking or what I am looking for. Perhaps it doesn't exist. Perhaps he was never cursed like the rest of us. And then... as I watch... from the corner of his right eye, the only one I can see, there comes... perfectly formed... a tear.

This house is becoming smaller. I thought it might be that I had grown but I can't remember a time when I would have felt anything less than discomfort in here. It is too dependent. It exists by a mere technicality. The old house, if a thing fell off, you nailed it right back on. I should nail a shingle or a tile and stop this constant, plastic whisper of escaping air.

But the jellypatch only fits the cloth.
It will only hug into the fibres
While I live in the shadows where she cannot find me.
Where the walls are firm
And not treacherous
For I am Alexei
And I am waiting
For tigers

Alexei

I close my eyes and refuse to participate in their game of rumour and conjecture. Behind my eyelids the memory of snow appears as white and unassuming as an inevitable conclusion, and I tell again to myself what I refused to them... that I am here to exorcise my tiger.

I did not know that when I came. It was an answer that I found along the way, in a trap, waiting for me to find it and be seduced by the freshness of its appeal.

That being the way of all lies...

I read the English poets while learning that, just a short distance beyond the city, away over the clambering bridge to where snow falls in silence, there is another tiger; white and stark, steaming breath into sharply symmetrical air, damaging it with patterns and movement the like of which Blake could never have imagined.

I close my eyes against the blinding white of my memory... and step back in time.

I stalk her. Watch her. Watch her sensing me.
See the blood in the spoor.
Hear the rumble deep within.
Move on.
And follow in the dance.

Then and now I understand that I was just a tool being sharpened, no more, and in this small, cramped house there is space only for a man. No room for tigers.

Take this small house.
Place it on the top of a tall tower.
Spring the trap.
Watch it leap
Paint red through the clouds
Leaving tracks like
Blood in the spoor

For three days the snow has fallen; soft feathers torn from the whitest of geese. The traps I set, buried and deep. Above the snow-hole the air is clean and crisp. Whites wash into pale blues at the horizon.

The tiger within me awakes. I feel her walk amongst me. I look inside and find evidence of her intervention. The inside of my skin cloven by her marks. Old. New. Scarred and once thought forgotten. She has been with me always. Though only in this last three days have I come to know her.

I close my eyes.

And I can see her now...

And a stark memory... of home...

Momma? Momma?

She replies with silence.

I ask again. Why is the man from the Party here?

I am not sure, she says.

Momma? What have I done?

She is laying washing over a chair back, trimming the folds between fingers marked with red, like frost marks, like ice-trapped skin. But I know them to be warm and beneath the hard surface they are gentle and whatever I have done cannot take that away, only make it harder to find.

We must wait until he has finished with Papa, she says.

Voices in another room.

I see Papa's head through the curtain, moving slowly back and forth, determined, hands raised… a cry of incredulity.

Momma! Momma! What is he saying?

The cloth falls naturally into flat squares upon the table. Chenille, the colour of blood. Squares picked out in bright white cotton. Stitching like fresh tracks in snow. Rose in the centre. Red.

Patience, munchkin

Blood in the spoor
It is her season
And because of that
I know her name

I crawl from the snow-hole. Suddenly the sky is huge. The sun sears the ridge, hammers the endless million crystals and at the edge of my vision she is white, bordering yellow with age, striped dark in the lee of rocks, asymmetrical, breaking, snow-field fresh and low. Her eye is hard and bright.

I stay silent. Hoping she will come to me. For I have little left with which to follow. Tracks hopelessly lost. This must be my last day. After that, I will become just another mark in the snow. And no-one will know these things that I have discovered out here.

And inside

I put the sun to my back. Slide along the shadow. Check my watch and compensate for rotation and the hour. Tilt the edge of my hand like a sight. Line up the marks. There. The last trap. Less than five hundred metres west, beyond a faint line in the flat of the field, not thirty metres from the edge of the forest where Korean pine soars black into the sky and the feet of Sika deer patter needles underfoot. I get up. The snow sucks at the laces of my boots.

Kisses the soles

Lingering

Slowing

I find her marks in the snow and turn to follow them, knowing what I will find. She has heard the sound of struggle, watched the dance of a loosening soul with a quiet, patient eye. Knowing that just by being there she was making a mark.

The trap is empty. Almost. The head of a snow hare severed against the wire at the bottom of the hole. And the scent... that hard, pungent scent of tiger. I dismantle the trap. To kill without wanting is abhorrent to me. She is always wanting. That may be a trap in itself. I strip the white fur from the head and sit down to wait.

I study the hare's skull in my gloved hands. Under the fur there are small slivers of flesh. Raw. Bloody. Along the cheeks are muscles that once chewed roots, tubers, soft spring shoots; teeth now broken and blunted on the unforgiving wire. I turn the head. It smiles at me. Sardonic. And I think of Ivaan. The way he has become...

We fall together inside an aeroplane. Feet and hands flailing. Mouths wide. Gasping. Laughing. Holding down the contents of our stomachs. He reaches out and grasps my hand. His fingers, elegant, slender, retrousse-tipped, curl around mine. We tumble together. Ivaan holds me tight. I push away. A smile. A hidden smile. Regret. I close my mouth and the laughter stops. We swim air in silence. Looking inwards. For possibilities. For traps. Sketched briefly in the air.

By a smile. I reach down inside and grab the tiger. We touch. I take his hand. As a man. He nods. Understanding. He reaches out. Embraces me briefly. Kisses both my cheeks. As a man. The tiger retreats...

The hare's rictus reminds me of the traps of my life; always emptied before I can reach them so that I can be... what? Alone?
But how can a man be alone
When within him
There is a tiger

I turn my head and she is watching me.
For one still moment
I exist in a world
Juggled by a madman

Alexei

I shuffle this fragile house down into the dust of the hollow beneath my back and wait. For this small world to go around. With me fastened to the outside and soon to be at the bottom and waiting.

Waiting for the hammer of the sun.

Is there anywhere else in the universe where the sun rises an incredible emerald green? And yet emeralds are fateful, jealous stones; glittering in the eyes of small gods and eternal women, riding the edge of a ring like a spiteful spark flung from the celestial carousel. I pull the filter into place as the sun climbs the horizon.

Out there somewhere is Boris in the Orbiter. Criticising with an intelligence that flows in and out through the tips of his fingers.

Balancing the powers.

How lucky his women should be...

Boris

'Ivaan?'

I wait. A minute. Then a minute longer, perhaps no more. Suddenly the radio cracks with static.

'Boris?'

'Here.'

'What can you see?'

I look at the screen and I can see nothing. It swirls with dust. Interspersed with flashes of red and green.

'Probably less than you.'

'The blister. What can you see from the blister?'

My fingers tingle as from them flow attitudes and rotations. Spinning. Checking. I get up from the chair.

I brace my feet in the docking ring and carefully lift an edge of the filter.

'Christ, Ivaan!'

'Tell me what you see!'

'What have you done?'

'I've done nothing. Tell me what you see!'

Above the approaching horizon a vast cloud of dust hovers in space. A film of green writhes across it like angry lightning. The edges of the cloud are tucking in, mushroom-like, and the stalk is spreading as if it were rooted deep into the surface; its tendrils breaking the dust halfway around the lit pathway of this tiny world-let, drawing it in, creasing it with knotted veins of deepest emerald.

'I'm not sure. I think the whole place is shrinking. Get out of there now!'

'I can't.'

'Why? Grab Kalenikov and get the hell out of there!'

'I don't know where he is.'

'Then get out without him!'

'I think he's still attached.'

'You think? You don't know?'

'He's not answering.'

'Then he's not attached.'

'You sure?'

'No.'

Kalenikov. Imperious. Cossack. Bastard. How many times has he refused to acknowledge us? Five months is time enough to lose count.

'What's he doing?'

'He detached the lance from the Egg. Said I was clumsy. Told him the struts locked me in. Wouldn't hear it.'

'There's only enough waste air in the lance for fifteen minutes. How long has he been out there?'

'Half an hour. He tapped into the cabin oxygen. Said we only needed five minutes to get back and dock.'

'But what's he doing?'

'I'd cleared an edge of the plinth. The gas seeped out from under it. Slowly at first. Then it came like a geyser. Alexei took the lance and blasted the edge away, opening up a gap under the plinth. The gas hurtled out around us and for a moment it was clear. I saw him. Moving along the edge. Playing the lance. Digging and digging with the gas streaming and swirling in coils around him. And he was laughing... I couldn't hear him but I know he was laughing. Then the dust closed in around us again. For all I know, he's still out there digging.'

Alexei

They think I'm digging but my hands are still and cradled. And in my memory the severed head drips rawness through the fingers of my gloves. I watch her draw back. Winding the energy into a trap from which she will spring.

I look inside myself and see that I know her. I have always known her. She watches my eyes, looking for fear. And finds only her name.

I smile. My lips draw back and show her that I too have teeth. I watch her eyes flicker. There is a lessening. The tension falls from her. She steps towards me.

Pauses

Bridging

She waits. Her presence in the air that surrounds us is immaculate.

I feel the soft rumbling of life inside her. It spills across my face. Her bright, acrid breath excites me. She stops. Her eyes are fixed. Immobile as stars. Then for a moment they flicker. They take in the raw blood that spills across my hands, then return to mine. She waits. I reach down inside to where my own tiger waits. In one swift movement I embrace it. Forgiving, I see the marks. And now I see the pattern they make. And the pattern is… myself. And now I know who I am, I am filled with a calm that transcends all things.

As I sit

And face
The final tiger

I hold the head between us. She reaches with the softness of her mouth, bereft of threat, and takes it from my outstretched hand. I reach up and catch a whisker. Nip between forefinger and thumb. She pulls away gently and I have it. I slide it, stiff as a needle, into the space between the stitches in the collar of my parka.

I close my eyes
And know
That I am the first
On such a day
For tigers

Boris

'Ivaan. The gauges. Are they still dropping?'

'Yes… wait… no, they've stopped.'

'Then for Christ's sake get him back in there and lift off.'

'Not possible. I can't cycle the airlock.'

'It's not damaged?'

'No.'

'Are the gauges still dropping?'

'No.'

'Ivaan!'

'They're at zero. I only have my suit supply.'

'Then get back up here now.'

'What about Alexei?'

'Leave the stupid bastard! I need you now. We need the Egg's shield for re-entry. And you know it takes two pairs of hands.'

'Wait! I can see him!'

'Where is he?'

'He's still out there. Pounding at the edge of the plinth with the empty lance. The end is bent and twisted and he keeps pounding it into the crack under the plinth.'

'What does he think he's doing? Get out of there!'

'Wait! It's opening up. The edge is falling inwards. God! It's hollow! I can see right inside. It's all hollow! Like a Fabergé egg. I'm sliding. No, I'm not! It's the plinth. Tilting!

The boulder! Oh, Jesus Christ! My legs... Boris. My legs. My...'

'Ivaan... I'm losing you. Five seconds and gone. ETR thirty minutes.'

' ... I'll... be here...'

No word from Kalenikov.

By the time I get back the dust will have settled. I hope Ivaan will sit quietly. Do as he's told. I can already feel Kalenikov working himself into impatience. There's something strange there. I've seen it, and it's easy to put a name to out here...

On Darkside.

Ivaan

As a family we are softly academic. Resting inside the long reach of Mother's arms, more poverty than poor. For that, perhaps, I shall blame my father. But it is too easy to paper the cracks of his curiosity.

As Mother so often says after describing his faults and shortcomings in the greatest of detail.

'Ivaan, where else should I want to be?'

And while I wait for Alexei to explain, in all his wisdom, why he has decided to kill me, none of these secrets will matter. Neither the hiss of air from the suit nor the constant distortion of the Egg as it collapses under the weight of the boulder can wring any change from the past that accompanies me...

We live our life through books, in winter quite literally; Mother feeds the stove because Father cannot tear himself away from his consuming desire for study long enough to go out and find something different to burn.

He doesn't know that we are burning them. We take them from behind the piles until the front rows hide empty-hulled cases.

Father goes to collect food and always comes back with another book to add to the row. We sully the names of a hundred loaned-to and non-returning relatives when he can't find the ones he wants because we have warmed our hands against the glow of their dissembling words and ink.

Mother justifies this by saying that once a book is written... it remains written... and despite being burned it can never be undone.

And I read every word that we burn. I speak their names as the flame takes them into smoke and whisper them against the ceiling in my sleep and here they sit buried deep in my useless brain waiting for... what? And out of all these words that I take in through my eyes and inhale deep into the very centre of my being, only one remains worthy of memory. And that word is...

And still I wait for Alexei to tell me why, and back at the Academy my mother will be shopping. In shops without queues. Shops that have 'things' on the counter and not just the odd one or two buried beneath the marble top waiting like words in smoke for that special customer.

Because I am here.

And so, because of a lie, because of a secret that we shared and kept from my father, but only I take with serious intent, I have become the Word.

Every word I have ever read I remember with such perfect clarity that I could not consciously stop thinking of them, until Boris taught me how...

Alexei

I open my eyes. From within the tiger's jaw the hare stares back at me, close as the hand at the end of one outstretched arm, yet somehow I see nothing incongruous in this. She lifts her lips. They curl back over yellow, distended incisors, held apart only by the fragility of the skull between them, to show me the acceptance in the dark orbits of its eyes. The teeth close the gap. The hare disappears. There comes the faintest of sounds.

Perhaps one we hear only at the point of death.

She rises to her feet. Her hugely distended belly drags in the snow and sways as she moves. Her breath is quicker now, beating my face with the wings of her internal heat, the air fetid and acidic.

She turns away and I realise that
For as long as a minute or more
I have forgotten how to breathe

She lurches suddenly, swings around, tracks away to the east, ungracefully stumbling. I allow her perhaps twenty metres then follow her descent towards the river, leaving the pines behind us to darkly rim the wide horizon. Her track becomes a slur across the blanket of snow where her belly rides the small ripples and blown shadows of sparkling frost. Closer to the river my feet sink deep into the softer layers. I pause as she tracks sideways beside the water's edge. Beyond the river, rocks dot the landscape, visible only by the irregularity of the shadows they cast.

Within four hundred metres the rising ground blurs against the white of the sky as though it is just another step upwards, leading me away from Earth. Halfway to the top of the ridge is an overhang of rock, dark shades inhabiting the space beneath. I see her earlier tracks leading down from there to the river.

She drags herself along the edge of the flowing water to where it narrows. She stands a moment. I see her body shudder with a contained violence. She twists in a spasm of pain and in two swift strides she is across the river and retracing her steps towards the overhang.

I move down to the waterside, staring up to where unrelieved white meets white broken only by the stripes of her fur. I watch as she turns around and around, flattening the snow with broad pads. A contraction shakes her body like a sudden wind, gusting her sideways until she falls out of sight into the hollow.

Spaced across the river are two rocks. One bears the wet print of the tiger, the other untouched by her leap. In this situation I trust her instincts more than my own, yet I cannot do this in two strides. And if I fall in the river I will die. From higher up the ridge I hear an agonizing groan and in an instant know why I am here. I look inside once more and see the tiger within me. I grasp it tightly and leap. The dry rock tips and ripples under my foot, my weight shifts suddenly forward as my ankle turns and cracks, I ignore it and use the momentum of my falling to propel me to the next one.

My foot fits neatly over the tiger's print and I pause, balancing on one foot with the bank one and a half metres away. Without further thought I collapse myself inwards, then explode into a one-footed leap over the water to land face down on the bank. I roll over and away from the danger of the river, coating myself in soft, glistening snow. I sit up to catch my breath and examine my ankle. It moves easily, if painfully, therefore it can't be broken... I tell myself.

On all fours I follow the trail up to the overhang. Below the edge of the hollow I turn and wait until my heart ceases to pound and breath sits more easily in my chest. My extended feet frame the blackly flowing river below. The thrumming pain of my ankle reminds me that I cannot easily return the way I came.

I listen to her breath. Constricted by each contraction taking place inside her belly it is harsh and rasping. Occasionally, a childlike whimper escapes her, but I am convinced this is just a fancy of my own imagination. I drag myself to the lip of the hollow and peer over.

The snow in the small depression is melted by the amniotic fluid that has poured from her body. Her rear quarters splay across the darkly spreading patch. Her breath is rapid now, pumping pain into the frosty air where it congeals.

I watch the convulsions track along her belly and wait for the first cub to appear. They track with ever greater urgency. Her breath showers me with brilliant mist.

Suddenly, she spasms; exquisite violence displays across her whole body, her lips draw back as she bites the bitterness from the air, her paws slash a futile wind across my face. She makes to stand then collapses back into the hollow. Beaten, her breathing slows. I watch the convulsions recede. She moves; sluggishly, indolent. Her limbs begin to shake. Her head turns towards me and I see the light leaving her eyes. Her legs are stilled as all movement fades from her. I clamber over the edge and slide into the hollow.

I touch her. She remains motionless. Her warmth reaches into me through my parka and all I want to do is struggle in beside her and allow it to soak through me as if it were a river of heat flowing between us.

I close my eyes for a moment and take the time to consider why I have followed her.

Ivaan

Walking in front of me is Alexei. I hurry to catch him but he hears my footsteps and strides out in a manner I can never match with my own hesitant step.

I settle back to my thoughts and watch his back, the way the coat folds against his shoulder blades as his arms swing, generating heat inside our bodies as we have been taught, and I imagine the skin stretching soft over the hard interior and the shape of his back and the slender twist of muscle as he bends and turns and I am content to watch... for now.

Five years at the Academy and I remain fascinated by these simple things, the steam that escapes each time I leave the apartment block to cross the wide empty streets; the way the ice cracks beneath my boots as I walk along repeating yesterday's lesson in my head, extrapolating from what I already know until today's lesson sits there before me, apparent and ready.

Once inside I settle to observe him, two rows in front and three places to the left and from here I can see the side of his pale cheek and the lift of an arched eyebrow as he begins to understand. I already have a page written and sit there ticking off my assumptions as they fall correct.

Boris sits to my right, shaking his head in annoyed wonder. I know he struggles with words. His skin is swarthy and even now this youth bears black hairs along the ridges of his knuckles; wisping out from under the sleeves of his jumper. He holds up one hand in self-disgust as again he misses the point and that hand is short and wide like the blade of a shovel, yet those fingers have a life of their own once near switches and keyboards. He says he doesn't think. He just does. And it is right. He has no wish to explore that in case, with understanding, comes the loss of the facility. And he would die first. I see already that he will die later, but I do not tell him. Because I know it would not change him.

At lunch I pick a table from where I can see Alexei. I watch his strong fingers tear at the bread with a generous sweep of hands that can stem only from farm life, where queues are what cows form waiting to be milked and bread is something baked from the last fresh crop of wheat; the leaving of soup in the bowl, of potatoes at the side of the plate where there will always be more tomorrow.

Boris sits down across from me. I shift in my chair so that I can still see Alexei. Boris shifts again to block my view, in the way that he does to Alexei when he smiles at his mother. Poor, solitary Boris. His mother and the stars. Those are his boundaries, he says. He already has the one, and he just needs to reach out for the other.

'I want to ask you something,' he says. I reassemble the food on my plate into rows, peas stacked like books, carrot wheels ranking in a library of sustenance as I wait for the words I know are coming.

'How do you do it?' he asks.

I shrug, 'Duty.'

'Duty?'

I empty the shelf of potatoes, hiding the exposed white of the plate beneath a veneer of green vegetable mush, 'There is a responsibility in words.'

'Explain,' he says.

I re-order the plate so that it still looks full despite what I have eaten, knowing that the illusion will collapse as suddenly as my father's when the Party took me from the local school and, deciding to accept the offer to move here with me, he ordered cases by the dozen only to discover when he began to pack that he had lived inside of a lie and not felt its tentacles of untruth. And now I am his Library. On quiet evenings when the Academy is closed and his unquenchable thirst for reason demands a knowledge that I hold inside of me, I reassemble the words into the ones he wishes to hear.

Boris taps the edge of my plate with his knife and I am forced by my conditioning to respond.

'Words shape our present. We are what we know and hear and from that we define ourselves.'

I return to the contemplation of the library on my plate.

He taps again, 'So?'

'So… with words we can reconstruct the past. Not only can we stand on the shoulders of giants but we can also describe them in great detail.'

'But they are shoulders nonetheless,' he says.

The carrots are now hiding the lack of peas that previously hid the lack of potato that covered the white of the plate and I see that the illusion is on the point of collapse and Boris says,

'And from these great shoulders, what can you see?'

'Words,' I reply.

'And what use is that if words already exist and have done so forever in your 'reconstructed past'?'

'With words, we can also construct the future.'

He sits back in his chair and briefly studies his hands, shaking his head slowly, 'I make my own future,' he says, 'In fact, it is already made.'

I reply, 'Then you need only to enact it for the audience.'

'And what do you see as my future?' he asks.

I collapse the construct on my plate and leave nothing but
the white of the porcelain,
    'You shall have your stars.'
    He smiles… until I say,
    'And they shall have you.'

Alexei

In the smallness of night behind my eyes I see my father. I am five years old and he is tall and magnificent and in the stall beside us is a cow. Her belly is heavily swollen and she is bellowing in pain. I begin to cry. He pats my head with a hand, dripping blood-streaked fluid into my hair.

'Don't cry Alexei…' he says, gently, 'It is her time. This is the way things are. Sometimes we all need a little help. When there are things we cannot do on our own it is no shame. Remember that.'

He turns away and reinserts his arm deep into the rear of the cow.

'This new baby needs a hand to help him turn.'

I remember his smile then.

'Perhaps he is a little awkward. Like you, eh? Wait here and see.'

His arm begins to reappear, his hand suddenly glistening into view, clutching two legs thin as parlour candles and seemingly twice as brittle. He places one hand on the rump of the cow and pulls hard on the legs, effort stitching across his face and shoulders, tuning the muscles of his arm into ridges and hollows tracked by veins standing as sharp as the river that now runs silently below me.

Ivaan

Boris moves aside and I see that Alexei has gone, and with that my heart sinks. He taps my plate to snatch me back into his presence,

'If you know all the words that exist, can you not create a new order?'

'That is what we do when we predict the future,' I reply.

'And how do you stop yourself from knowing?' he asks, 'What if you see your own future and do not like it?'

'Does it matter what I like?' I reply, 'What difference would it make? I am an observer, not a mechanic.'

'That sounds like religion,' says Boris.

'Yes, it does,' I reply.

'And who is your mechanic?'

'I have no broken parts,'

'Yes... you do,' he says.

I smile and sit back as his fingers twirl the cutlery, flashing the air with the neon of the canteen lights.

I wait.

Eventually he stops and pauses for a moment, then leans forward conspiratorially,

'Your 'Off Switch' is broken.'

'I have no 'Off Switch'.'

'And there is the fault,' he says, 'but don't worry, I have the answer.'

From under the table he draws a slim folder, reaches in and twitches free a slender, hard-covered book. He places it softly on the table and covers it with flat, blade-like hands; hands I have seen his mother rubbing oil into when the cold and ice have cracked open the skin and her touch is at once raw and soothing in his eyes.

Reaching out across a remembered bar room table she takes hold of mine,

'You too should use the oil I give him,' she says.

I in turn study the hands holding mine, and find them soft and unlined as if they have never encountered hard work, which they have not, and as if they have lived their life soaked in some kindness of fluid which has not allowed them to age, and from there to her face aglow with buried youth in the dim light and wonder how she looked at thirteen when she gave birth to Boris, and why no-one had bothered to record that event with even a simple camera or a sketch.

Boris taps my plate again,

'I want you to take this book,' he says, 'and tonight, when you are alone, I want you to read it like it was one of your father's books… and then burn it.'

I reach out but he presses down emphatically on it, squeezing out the air from between the pages, 'Do not open it now, only later, when you are alone. For in these pages lies your future… as I see it.'

In the corridor I see Alexei leave the toilet and so I enter, searching the empty cubicles for one containing his residual warmth. In the third, the cistern is filling. I close the door and sit down on the fading body-heat of the seat. I close my eyes and hold the book close to my chest and press down hard on my self-disgust at what I am doing. When had I fallen so far?

I hold out the book but cannot bring myself to open it in case Alexei should leap out from within the pages and devour me with his unseeing, non-committal eyes and his strong shoulders will not allow me to press the pages back together again.

For the rest of that afternoon I cannot move my eyes from the book. I study the shiny red whorls of the cover, the ramrod spine and the delicacy of the individual gold-leafed edges. For three hours I look at Alexei not once. And in that three hours I find space for a small detachment, and am grateful to Boris.

And am still so.

I see that book as I sit here, trapped hard between terminal love and pragmatism, between one who makes me want to be… and one who has shown me how to. And forever out of reach of either.

As the vacuum sucks away every word of my father's I see that I shall be left with this that Boris presented to me. I have re-read that book many times in my head. It has been my salvation and my cross and now I see that it was the only one ever worth reading…

Alexei

I take off my left glove.

The cold bites fiercely at the tips of my fingers.

The sleeve of my parka will only withdraw to the wrist. This will not be enough. I slip off my pack and satchel and throw them onto the top of the overhang out of the way. I shrug my shoulders inside the parka and manage to withdraw my arm from the sleeve. I allow it to escape beneath the hem. The cold is incisive. A slight movement of wind showers needles through the fabric of my knitted jumper.

I manoeuvre myself behind the tiger, pinning her tail to one side with my other elbow. I fold the fingers of my hand like the petals of a tulip. Thankfully, she is still leaking fluid. Inside her, the heat is unbearable after the searing cold. It feels wrong, invasive, demeaning… and entirely intimate. There are vague flashes of sexuality, faint urges shimmering like collected images in the back of my mind.

The face of my father flickers into being, smiling, arm sunk umbilically deep into a cow and I see at once how the smile came into being as my vision transfers to my fingertips and I feel the cub warm and soft but intrinsically still under my touch… I feel a cord, wound around a small neck, out between front legs and attached somewhere within. I push beyond it into a space filled with movement, the small beating of hearts, the frustration and urgency of tiny fragile limbs.

I retreat again and allow my fingers to do their work.

Untwisting the cord I take hold of the cub and turn it in my hand until the legs follow my fingers out into the riveting cold. I lay it on the snow, fluid crystallising on my arm as I turn it over, prodding, teasing my fingers into its ribs to feel... nothing. I lay it respectfully to one side and reinsert my hand, the heat again as searing as the cold. The other three cubs have moved closer to the neck of the womb.

Their cords are clean and aligned.

I withdraw my hand, shrug myself back into my parka and put back my glove.

Kneeling beside her, I listen to her breathing. While I have been working it has become shallow and irregular, sometimes stopping for a few moments before starting again. The convulsions have disappeared. She has given up, defeated by the violence of stilted birth and as I watch her slip away I think of the things I have achieved and all the things I have yet to achieve and of the mountain of fear I have climbed just to be here beside her, but more than that, just to discover myself.

There is a righteous anger growing inside me. I feel it begin in shame, be propelled through loss to rocket through what might yet be... until it erupts from my throat in a roar that astounds me. I lift my arm and bring it crashing down on her ribs. Again and again. Until she stirs... shudders her breath back into being. A convulsion shakes her, brilliant and painful behind her eyes.

Three cubs slither out onto the snow between her legs in a cascade of fluid warmth. She waits a moment, filling her lungs deeper and deeper until she can raise her head. Turning, she noses them into the warm shadow of her belly, growls vaguely as I lean over and pull away the cauls.

I drag myself around to reach up for my pack and satchel and drop them down onto the packed snow. I open the flap and pick up the dead cub. I dangle its legs over the opening of the bag. She looks up at me, then sharply away, her eyes expressionless. I hesitate. She looks up at me again. I push the cub in amongst the others and stare back at her. I fold the flap shut and strap on my pack.

My ankle is painful but seems bearable... until I try to stand. I take out my knife and cut a webbing strap from the empty satchel and wind it around my ankle, reinforcing the top of my boot. I loop the end, insert the handle of the knife and twist until I cry out with pain. This is the best I can do. And sometimes that is all that is left to us.

I rotate onto my knees and stand, using my good left leg to prise me from the snow. She turns her head and snarls menacingly at the movement, before her eyes fall to her belly where three cubs nestle against her teats, mewling and jostling for the warmth and milk. The fourth lies silent, stiffening rapidly.

I withdraw the whisker from my collar and place it gently on the back of the dead cub.

It is enough that I know.

I turn to face the sun as it begins its slow descent towards the filtering pines... beyond the river.

Ivaan

The camera is still working and I see Alexei where he sits against the edge of the tilted plinth. There is a green-ness about him. So far it covers only his legs but it appears to be growing, moving around behind him. It is somehow indefinable, more a suggestion of green than a deliberate dye. I think at first that it is from his boot trace then I remember that his is red,

'Blood in the spoor...'

and mine is gold.

My left leg and arm are outside the egg through a fold in the broken shell and although I can't feel them, I imagine that if I try I can reach just far enough to touch him, to tap him, like Boris on the edge of my plate that long ago afternoon and with a simple gesture draw him into my presence, to take away this sense of loneliness that the lack of words has left behind in its place.

'Alexei?'

'What...' he replies, flatly.

'Did I ever tell you about Boris's book?'

Silence.

'Tiger-man!'

'I hear you.'

Alexei Kalenikov... how do I love him? Now that he has killed me.

'I hear you too…'

The Egg creaks around me. But all I want to hear is silence. And my own heart beating in my throat. Alexei. Alexei. Alexei…

'…you bastard.'

'A misjudgement.'

'Is that your way of making an apology?'

Silence.

'Damn you! I demand to die by catastrophe. Not by mistake.'

My legs are disappeared beneath a metal bulkhead. Folded, rivets sprung out in collapse, the curve of the boulder shears the metal. It is marked where the hull has torn lines deep into its surface and I wonder if that is where the pain exists.

For I feel none in here…

'Cossack!'

Silence.

'Bastard.'

A portal ring pulls into my side as the boulder settles its mass gracefully under low G. My left arm is pinned where the hull folds across it above the elbow. The suit is twisted there like a tourniquet. My hand is exposed to the vacuum and although I cannot see I can still imagine the unspeakable happening out there. All I feel is cold. And this thing all twisted up inside of me. Not knowing what it is. The secrets. The listening. And I cannot scratch its surface.

'Tiger-man.'

Silence.

I wait. The pulse ticks on in my throat. Timing is everything. When one has something to give that must not be returned.

Suddenly… 'Ivaan?'

I bite my tongue. I have reached out before. And been made to understand. Above all other times, this time is mine. I must become... a tiger. How would she move? With stealth? Without fear? No. There is always fear. It may be masked but ever present. With care. With caution. With great skill and deliberation.

This is my season...

'Ivaan...'

I wait. The time is not yet. The cold seeps further into my arm. Something strange happens. I feel my toes again. I move them. Up and down. The bulkhead hides my legs at some impossibly refracted angle like brushes in a water jar. I close my eyes into blackness. I open them. It stays. I move my toes on hidden strings.

I dance my legs as the helmet horrors rise inside me. Strings thrum against my cold fingers... faster... faster. Outside, vacuum bursts the flesh. Nails lift and bleed. The blood boils and congeals. The skin rips at every fold. I burst forth, dancing into the airless void around me, sowing my life in manic rows; neatly tended, ploughed, drilled, harvest ready and waiting for the sun. Here! I even bring my own water! Watch it flow. Warming the soil...

I scream, 'Bastard!'

No! Not yet. I push the horrors back down. This, is not the way. Within any season, there is a special time.

If I can only wait.

'Ivaan.'

'Fuck off!'

'Ivaan!'

Suddenly I know I can't wait.

'Alexei... I love you.'

'Ivaan... I can see it.'

Silence.

Inside the blackness, that silence becomes a howl of broken thoughts; rushing, unbidden, cascading. I jerk my legs again. Suddenly I'm running. The wide blue Georgian sky rushes down to fill my lungs and the grass flies beneath my feet. Sheep swoop and flock around me like lofted birds; undulating, borrowing their lift from the lush lee of the rolling land. They escape me. I chase their cloud shadows across the bright shallow slope.

My legs jerk again.

I am the wind.

My passing shakes the silver birch trees and leaves them rooted in their slow race for the sun.

I am a storm travelling the horizon. Striking down into valleys. Crossing waters. Sparkling. Thundering the steppe with footfall. Bending the grass like a summer rain.

I stumble. Strike the stony water and lie. Legs immersed. Left arm struggled beneath a large stone. Growing cold. My lungs hurt. They pump and pump. Drowning, I shake my head. The fingers of my right hand release the emergency oxygen. It seeps into my helmet. I awake into a greater horror. A blackness inside my head.

'Alexei?'

'Ivaan?'

'What… what can you see?'

'Nothing now. I think it was the Orbiter.'

'Can Boris hear us?'

'I don't know.'

'Then tell me that which you do know.'

'I only know one thing.'

'So do I.'

'Who I am.'

'You're a bastard. Let me in.'

Alexei… You're such a clever bastard. All I had was my speed. I ran after you so fast I was always out of breath. And you were never there when I arrived. Always somewhere else, like an insurgent chess-piece. And now the queen is in the castle and the castle is in ruins. Destroyed by a misjudgement. Your misjudgement.

'The King is fallible! Long Live The King!'

'Ivaan. Turn up your oxygen.'

'Fuck off, Your Majesty.'

'Ivaan, I…'

'Come out and fight, you Bastard King.'

'For what reason?'

'For Love.'

'Ivaan!'

'What's the matter, Alexei? Afraid?'

'It's not appropriate.'

'Not appropriate? You want my forgiveness, don't you?'

'No…'

Followed by silence, while I hurt so far down inside it feels like an external pain. As if my arm were trapped and my legs were crushed and the flesh of my hand and arm were exploding into space. What's that tapping? Tap tap tap tap.

'Get away from me you bastard. I can hear you tapping. Why are you tapping? Leave me alone. Get away from the Egg.'

The tapping has stopped. I close my eyes and imagine him walking away from the Egg, leaving slatted prints in the dust, a little jet of red dye ejecting from the sole of his boot with each step. They would have been gold from mine.

So we would know. They said.

Blood in the spoor. He said.

'I don't mind when I can't hear you. For four days I couldn't hear you. And you didn't know I was listening.'

'I knew.'

'Shut up.'

Silence.

'For four days while you went off to find your tiger. The whole thing was a joke... but you couldn't see it. I was the one person who knew why you'd gone. You'd gone to build a wall, to find the last few bricks to shield you against the rest of us. There was a great miscalculation...'

'Where?'

'On the part of the tiger... it should have fucking eaten you.'

'Then how would I have been able to hear what you are going to tell me.'

'Don't tell me what I'm going to do, you bastard.'

'You're going to tell me again that you love me.'

'Why should I? You would only hear it... when all I want you to do is listen.'

'Ivaan, I know...'

'What... that you're arrogant?'

'No... I know what was in the book that Boris gave you.'

'Why would Boris tell you of all people?'

'He didn't. I just know. I saw the look on your face.'

'You saw... me? You looked... you actually saw me...?'

'Ivaan... I have always seen you. Always heard. Always listened.'

'Then what was in the book?'

'Nothing...'

'Nothing?'

'Nothing is the only thing that either of us had to give you. I gave you nothing from the start but it was Boris who made the connection, who helped you to switch off so that you could become a part of us instead of being just a repository of meaningless text. Without the book you would not be here.'

'And inside the book?'
'The pages were blank.'

Alexei

The river clucks its tongue amongst the rocks and colls of the bank, spinning into sky-reflecting whorls beside minor obstructions. It is less than a metre deep, but deep enough to freeze in. The rock on which I twisted my ankle has rolled until its water-polished side is upwards. A haze covers it where air brushes the surface. The rock I shared with the tiger seems impossibly far beyond my reach.

I take the weight off my ankle by kneeling in the soft snow. I take up a handful and examine it. It is heavy, crystallised by the moist air down by the river into an almost transparent mesh. I hold it to the sun and watch as the light filters through it into sharp blues, indigos, flashes of indescribably bright yellow. I heft it in my hand, then slip the pack off my shoulders and shuffle to an unmarked area.

I stand on one foot, swing my arms, windmill my way into a leap. As I hit the floor again my ankle collapses beneath me and I roll to a stop.

The effort has awoken the pain. It burns with a cold fire that seeps upward along my leg where spasms rip my calf muscles; tendons, charged like unbridled electrified wire, tear with every move. If this had been the river I would now have perhaps five minutes before all breath left me.

I look up at the sun to see that it is falling. I make my way back to the pack and empty it quickly onto the snow. There is nothing left of any consequence. What good are spare socks, containers emptied of food? I pile them up as a marker.

I consider the straps and ties. There is little of use. I slide the whole pack over my damaged foot and try to stand, using the straps in my hand as support, then sit down again rapidly and begin to laugh out loud, remembering the time my father had stood me in a milk pail, aged three, passed me the handle and told me to pick myself up.

I slip the pack off my leg and examine the breather holes. With the straps held up high, they will be over half a metre above my foot. I think back to the tiger, where one was sacrificed for the good of the many, and make the decision that has been staring me in the subconscious for the last half hour.

I slide the pack over my good leg and slither to the riverbank. Without hesitation I slip my damaged foot deep into the black water. The pain becomes a howl in my brain that settles to a whimper in my throat as the synapses begin to cancel out the signals pounding upwards from my ankle.

How long should I wait? How long does it take for the circulation to slow and stop? I count to sixty, then sixty more before I test it. I press down tentatively, then harder, until I realise I am already standing with one foot in the river and can feel nothing. I lower my other leg into it. The water reaches almost to the breather holes of the pack. If I am careful, and slow, I can do this. I lurch my damaged ankle further into the stream. If there are rocks under my feet I can't feel them, only the shifting of my balance as I slip and slide, but this body is my machine. I know the way it works.

Before my brain reawakens to the concept of time I have reached the other bank. I collapse gratefully onto the snow and slip the pack off my leg. Dry. I turn my back to the river and limp towards the pines.

Once inside the shelter of the forest I sit down against a tree. The ground is softened by a carpet of needles. There is a scatter of seeds and small pieces of timber and the footprints of deer where they have gnawed the bark from the lower branches.

To my left the sun is filtering through the boles of the trees, showering the forest with horizontal light, capturing the mist escaping from my mouth as I catch my breath. I stand up and lurch hopefully towards the point where it will soon disappear below the horizon.

An hour later and night begins to spread upwards along the tree trunks like a rising of waters. The leaf canopy is still lit and the light is golden on the matte underside of the needles. The trees soak it in, drawing it upwards, pulling on the skirt of darkness around me. Another half hour and I am in total night. I stumble on a few minutes more, hands held before me, blind without a stick, pain slowly returning to my ankle.

Close by me there are sounds of deer running unerringly through the forest with their black, hugely distended eyes, waiting for the moon but already seeing things that I cannot. Following them closely comes the crack of a rifle shot.

I stop as rapidly as if I have been struck. Twenty five metres away a torch sparks up a light between the trees and, in a moment of extreme courage, I begin to cry.

Ivaan

The cold of vacuum seeps up to my waist in small increments of negation. There is a swishing noise in my ears and I head-up the memory of a car with steamed-glass faces.

I watch Alexei wear his look of leaving like an escape. He sits back into the seat and relief washes him free as the car moves on and the ties drop away. But I see for a moment as one thing marks him.

The portal ring pressing my side begins to slip around me as the boulder settles deeper into the metal of the Egg. The movement stops.

'Ivaan?'

I will not dignify him with a reply. If ever a man should shut up and listen, it is Alexei Kalenikov.

'Ivaan?'

'Shut up.'

'Ivaan… I have known since the aeroplane.'

'Then why didn't you listen?'

'I heard. And understood.'

'I know you heard, you bastard. Why didn't you listen?'

'Because it was an unfamiliar word.'

'Love?'

'No. Uncertainty.'

'Love is never uncertain. Or it isn't love.'

'Yours is an uncertain kind of love. It works its way inside of a man and questions his beliefs. Ivaan, I know what I am, and your love is a flower of doubt that I cannot afford to nurture. It may blossom.'

'And so you shut me out along with the rest of the world, because we bring you into question? Go home, Alexei.'

'I would that I could.'

'Then go home in your head. To the time when you thought you were a farmer.'

'I never was a farmer.'

'Then become one. Watch the tyre tracks unroll behind you. Paint the fences. Clean the gutters. Listen to the old men singing and the clack of bone needles by the fire…'

'Ivaan…'

My helmet feels hollow inside. The cheeks of my face have become distended and swollen. My eyes pulse with an inner pressure and the helmet gauges are flat and level.

I pump for the last of the air.

'Let me in!'

'I can't.'

'Remember… you bastard!'

'I do remember.'

'Then will you listen?'

'…Yes.'

'Then remember your mother's last smile.'

Silence follows… and somewhere… lost in the deafening roar of that silence, I hear his heart break open.

I sense the blood in the spoor.

'That's how I love you.'

Alexei

Through a fold in the skin of the Lander, Ivaan's hand and forearm protrude. The palm is open and the fingers are torn and frosted. I reach up and take hold of his hand. Perhaps this was all he ever wanted. Perhaps I could have managed this much. I fold his shattered fingers in my own, curling them into a fist. Be angry, Ivaan. Be angry. If only I could have managed this much... maybe this is your catastrophe. I listen to his words and suddenly, I'm going home once more...

Papa opens the door. Climbs back up the ladder and soon I see gobs of earth falling, filled with autumn leaves in spring. There are seeds, caked with mud, rooting up there where the rain collects and groans down the pipes, swallowing sunlight and energy. Papa clears them all from the gutter, paints it lovingly with bright, sweet scented bitumens and creosotes; until the birds and the winds and the rains return. I look inside to see the marks these things have brought and laid upon me.

From off the roof a song begins; strong and lyrical. I see his feet from the window. The ladder racks the daylight sky.

Dark on light
Visible
Symmetrical

The car picks me up. Carries me away. Same car as before. Same mud spatter on black. Doors that open, bouncing, on little leather straps. Scooping a remnant of the farm air as it begins to move. Closing on Momma's tears. Papa looking frail. Leaning. Holding. Supporting. I cannot tell which. His arm is around her shoulders. She is smiling, pale and insignificant beside that which it hides. I think it will not last in my memory. And yet it has.

Inside the car is another boy. He is younger than I. But not much. A year perhaps. He says, hello, and smiles a wan smile that dances only around his lips. I nod. His name is Ivaan. Ee-vaan. Softer. We were Georgian, he says. I open my mouth to speak and find that my name is lost. I only know that I am special. I dare to ask the driver to slow. He halts by the gate. Ivaan's nervous fingers reach across the scallowed leather to touch mine. I move away as the weight of the day falls in through the closed windows and sits between us.

I see her face behind the curtains, then suddenly at the porch, on the path. Each picture slashing itself onto the inside of my eyelids. I see her face at the car window and I know she will hold me here if I stop to listen to the softness in her voice, to the language in her body. I keep it closed.

The car moves on.

Outside, there is a question shaped indelibly.

Why?

Inside, I have no answer.

Inside me there are no answers. Only marks. I look behind my eyelids. Ivaan smiles. I see it break and waver. Its tracks run silently down my cheek.

I see the house for the last time through a rain-streaked window and it seems as though I am stood still and the house stretching away into the distance like a part of me fastened to the earth and not yet capable of dislocation. I remember the tyre tracks. The tractor choking across the Collective's fields. Papa's hand on the wheel. The way it rolls beneath his touch. Unstoppable, he marks the swollen earth until it spurts high with birds black as tears from a hungry eye.

The car stops.

We dodge the rain to sit quietly on a train while the platforms and rails slide out from under us and the day recedes into the bright, white dot of a tunnel. We break daylight and watch the countless sheep freshly fallen across green fields. We devour it until it becomes embarrassing in its routine, its sameness. I stare from the train window and see the marks in their countless thousands.

The train stops at a grey station. We get off onto a platform under a sky shot with black and I listen to the engine sighing deep and onerous as if it has just put down a great burden.

We arrive at a checkpoint on the outskirts of a walled city. I look up to see a distant plume of silent flame shoot vertically into the cold, pale sky.

Doors close behind us.

The green line comes closer now. Like an early spring. The heat from the sun lifts the gas from the rocks and they become phosphorescent. It creeps across the surface, undulating over outcrops and sinking the hollows like a green pond scum, then recombines in the cold of the dark side. There are times, and now we won't ever know why, when it sways together as if a breeze has taken it. Like wind in the corn. Fresh and sassy.

The gas has grown to where my boots lay stretched out in the dust and I want to kick my feet in it, feel it cool between my toes and to get up and just run and run. Home...

I sit on the knoll to watch the tractor cough along by the edge as the sun takes the windows. I wink back at each one in turn as if we are sharing a secret that only the house and I understand. The grass pulls right over where I sit, like a new eiderdown quilt freshly sewn with squares and daisies and sheep floating in the void beneath me and I sink down into it and become part of it. I spin around and it coats me with its greenness.

I look down and the gas that covers my legs is specked with small intense white dots, like daisies. They are evenly spaced and move together with grace and determination.

I feel a wind blowing, teasing, through my mind...

There's a glow on the horizon. The gas is bright and thickening. I hit the com pad again.

Tum tum te tum

Tum tum te tum

Anything regular. Nothing random. Boris will be listening and know he is not alone.

The hiss of escaping air stops. The gas covers me now and I know that from above I'll look just like any other outcrop.

Suit Soup.

Ivaan joked about it on the way up, and now here I am ready for the croutons and the sprig of parsley. Which of the little-deaths comes first? The vacuum or the cold? Above me, stars stalk like tigers in black snow. I hold a breath in case they sense me waiting and I should lose them.

And I whisper to them

Rigel, Rigel,
Burning bright,
In the starfield,
Of the Night.

And I forget the little-deaths.

Boris

I sit and study my fingers to see them for what they have become. Purposeless appendages, forever flexing. Except now not forever. Forever is an animal that has escaped the zoo of my mind.

Suddenly the weight of my arms becomes indescribable. I try to lift them and find myself pressed against the world and wonder how I ever used them. I am no longer a man. I am a corpse waiting to cool.

The radio clicks and I am rebuilt as fingers track a familiar path.

'Ivaan?'

'Tum tum te tum, Tum tum te tum.'

'Kalenikov?'

'Tum tum te tum, Tum tum te tum.'

'Answer me!'

I reach out and switch off the radio and notice for the first time how it has been designed to fall under my hand. I wonder again at the ease with which I find these things. Even though the cabin has become redundant, still it hugs me to its lack of necessity like a dead infant to a dry breast.

Pointlessly, devoid of emotion, I type an empty header into the DataStream and press 'send'. The visuals from the camera have gone automatically. They will require no further comment.

I turn on the radio.

'Tum tum te tum, Tum tum te tum.'

Kalenikov. It can be no other. No one else has such manic, dogged persistence.

'Tum tum te tum, Tum tum te tum.'

No one else would fail to recognise the stopper on a Djinn bottle.

'Tum tum te tum, Tum tum te tum.'

I switch it off again.

I look out through the crystal of the blister and see that the dust has subsided. I can see where the boulder has crushed the Lander into the gap beneath the plinth, stopping the escaping gases. The skin of the asteroid appears to have stabilised, although it now appears aged, rutted like an old man's hand into veined heights and discoloured valleys. Perhaps that's what Ivaan was all along, the balance to Kalenikov, to stop him tipping the manic scale.

And now I know why I am here. Justice needs to be seen to be done. And now that it has, it no longer needs to be seen. And so I look up at the stars as Kalenikov wheels below and I know if I switch on the radio to entice the uselessness of my hearing, he will be there...

'Tum tum te tum, Tum tum te tum.'

And I will not listen. I will remember instead how it felt in the warm cradling dark from which Kalenikov had selfishly pushed her, my mother would slide into bed beside me.

Spooning herself to the warm shape of my back.

Her slender limbs

Careless

Sometimes forgetting

I ask my fingers for one last favour. In answer, they reach into the toolkit locker and return with an iron-tipped hammer.

I ask my arms once more to catch and hold the weight of what I am and raise the balance high. I tap once, sharply, on the crystal, and as it sprays away into the darkness I shout to the stars to come and join me. For within the knowledge that you are finite, there exists the loneliest place.

Alexei

The gas has entered my helmet through the hole where the aerial wire was pulled. I see it now, like an out of focus film. Pale and moving, the lights fall in through the gap.

They line up and I see them arrange before my eyes. I breathe the gas and nothing changes. Then I see them spiral open like umbrellas. Minute silk parasols. Their centres are gold and spinning, soaking up the light. They split as the sun comes over the horizon and hits my visor like a splendid hammer.

Out on the plain my Father's house rises from the dust. The shingles are green. The walls are green, pale as dust but the gutters and barges are bright and clean. It surmounts a knoll of green, glowing in sunlight like fresh, dew-ridden grass, sparked white with daisies.

There comes a song from the roof. The scuff of a broom in the yard. Metal shovel scraping over stones, hitting steps and large smooth pebbles brought back from the sea.

Fences, creaking and green in the new light. Steaming off the rain. Stretched out. Keening in the wind. Glistening in the dew and early sun. And all those lines pointing one way.

❄

The door hangs open.
The windows are wide and deep.
Within them is the comfort of a more solid darkness.
I stand up and the greenness cloaks me. The sun bends around me like a rod of molten gold.
I approach with silent footsteps. There is blood in my spoor. I place each one carefully into the ground until I reach the door. The house stands rigid, as if it is listening, then bows its head and continues with its quiet existence.
From deep within there comes a low rumble.

Alexei...
Enter...

The door is too small. I have grown since last I was here.

Take off your suit...

Then I will die.

The house will not notice. Enter...

I pause a moment, listening. And become aware that inside the house there is a smile waiting.

Beside me, a small gob of autumnal earth, filled with leaf, life and seeds, falls from the gutter.

Strong and lyrical, a song begins from the other side of the roof.

I flip the release and my helmet fills with the unmistakably sweet scent of bitumen.

And the sudden
Hard pungence
Of tiger

The Big Idea

Here is where we come back to one of my favourite themes... being seven.

One day, in Loutro on the sunny isle of Crete, I attended a workshop run by Bernadine Evaristo, a wonderful short fiction writer in her own right (write?)

The purpose of the exercise was to consider what we would say to our younger self if we could travel back in time.

Would we warn him/her about the girl/boy who would founder their teenage ship on the rocks? Would we give them financial advice? What indeed would we, or should we, warn them of.

I considered this for a while then began to write with the premise that if I went back with advice, and it was heeded, then perhaps I would not be sat here in the glorious sunshine considering this problem. I could be anywhere, in prison even!

Or I could have ceased to exist altogether.

Whatever transpired, I would not be me, and being me is not necessarily an unhappy thing. It has benefits, although I've not always been aware of them, and this project made me think harder than usual. I came up with a different solution. I began to look at the things we lose as we get older, acuity of thought and vision, the tempering of our expectations and the ability to think outside the box with that freshness of eye that comes with being seven.

So... instead of giving him something... I decided to borrow that eye...

The Big Idea

'Do I know you, mester?'

No, but you will

I watch his face twist with slow bewilderment. He turns around quickly, this way and that, never losing me from the corner of his eye.

'Where did you come from?'

I smile at the quiff his mother lovingly raises every morning. I see in the mirror the dark hair spilling out between her fingers, tucked by the comb. A quiet musty smell pervades his clothes and skin and I guess that here, now, it must be Thursday.

That doesn't matter

'Everybody comes from somewhere.'

I remember the check of the shirt he is wearing, know well how the blues and the greens would feel against my skin, the soft flannel of the short grey trousers with the hard ridge of doubled seam that I know is chiding his leg, making his crotch sore.

He shifts from foot to foot, rocking purposefully in the sunlight that spills into the yard from the lips of three-storey terraces, steaming attics crumpled with stale beds beneath glass-lights fastened shut to keep out a sudden rain.

Billy…

I register the slight shock that displaces the perennial smile.

Go… to the toilet

He hops, undecided, then streaks for the familiar door, third along the block with its neatly cropped pages of 'The Sheffield Star' pegged behind on a rusty nail.

While I wait I realise that I can't easily tell him how I know these things, or how to prepare himself for me. He returns amidst the sound of falling water and plants his feet square, slightly apart, in anticipation of the breadth of frame he will one day have. I reach out to touch the short sleeve of his shirt, checking my own memories, testing my age for symptoms. He steps away backwards.

Tell me a secret

He wonders, still smiling, guessing how deep he dare pass into the stream that runs beneath small boys where they sit on causeway edges, dangling their fresh imaginations into that flashing, caustic, dangerous fancy.

'Last Friday,' he says, coming closer with a shadowed, sideways twist, 'You won't tell my mom I telled you, will you, mester?'

Despite myself, and him, I let out a short, bitter laugh. The crumbling ochre brick and the stone-silent windows of the yard push it back at me.

I promise

He scuffs his feet, his gaze falling abjectly on the bared leather toes, the brogues with the too high sides that are irritating the scabs on his heel bones, the laces he has just worked out how to tie.

'Last Friday,' he says, '...my dad set fire to the chimney.'

I try hard to look surprised, but fail.

Is that your best secret?

He squints slyly at me, then spins on one foot, always out of reach.

'No.'

Then what is?

'It's *my* best secret.'

What is?

'If I told you then it wouldn't be.'

Do you tell your mom your secrets?

He shrugs, but I already know the answer.

His socks dishevel themselves heedlessly around his ankles, one three inches higher than the other, flagging up even now, at seven, the impending imbalance in his soul.

'Where *did* you come from, mester?'

He searches my face for things he might recognise.

What's more important, is where you're going to

I know that will be cryptic enough to trigger in him that lapsing, but insatiable curiosity.

'I can't go anywhere.' His toe stubs the concrete, a temporary, rolling hopelessness chastening his voice, 'My mom says.'

Where would you want to go?

I perch myself on the lid of a steel dustbin. He dances out of reach smartly, eyes left, then right, displaying an awareness that will soon restrict him to seek security above all else, colouring his life with the checks of his shirt, the thin red line of small successes, the blue of impending sadness, the green of the insidious jealousies that will fade but never wash clean in the 'Reckit's Blue' of his circumstance.

'I don't know,' he says, with a petulance as though I'd expected him to fall fully-formed and complete at my feet, 'Not yet.'

What if you never know?

'My mom says I will. She says…' and he slides his face up to the sun, where the slicing light touches and frames the memory of her words.

We speak them together,

'She says I'm full of Big Ideas.'

He stops, his smile for once frozen and impenetrable.

'What *are* you, mester?'

I think for a moment, then smile openly at my ability to retreat at will through the downward years.

I'm a Big Idea

He warms again at that, and I see the wall behind his eyes erode.

'I'm not scared.'

Should you be?

He pushes his hands deep into his pockets, withdraws the sea shell I know is there, turns it in his fingers, plunging one into the small pink ear before returning it to the one without the hole.

'Perhaps.'

Why should you be scared of an idea?

'Mom says mine will always get me into trouble.'

Hmm

I nod in agreement, watching him watching me.

'Will you get me into trouble, mester?'

Lots of it. And with a lot of people. But you'll survive

'Your eyes…' he says, 'They're the same as my moms. But your hair is silver… like my Granddad's. Does that mean you're old?'

He takes a step closer, leans in towards me as far as he dare. I back away a step.

'Do you know my mom?'

Yes

'Shall I fetch her?'

No...

How can I see her young again, knowing she will always be? Something inside me tears open and I drop through, a sensation of rope around my throat, a pressure of fluid hot behind my eyes.

No. I'm not ready to meet your mom. Not yet. Please don't tell her I was here. It can be our best secret

He looks me up and down, the faded jeans and the white tee shirt flagging up something for his attention.

'Are you a sailor?'

I think about that for a moment, the way I've arrived, the peculiar iridescent sea I've had to sail.

Yes

His eyes widen at the sight of my white deck shoes with no laces. I speak quickly then, before he takes me further down a road I am unprepared to travel.

So tell me your next-best secret

He looks around the yard furtively, then lowers his face into shade, his eyes becoming dark empty pools, his mouth small and quiet with shadow.

'...you wouldn't like me if I told you.'

I would...

'...You won't, honest, mester.'

I always will...

'...promise?'

And more...

'I... I killed something.'

A chill of memory streaks through me until it's fist of ice clamps around my heart. How can I have forgotten the sparrow? Fragile and fleeting, a grace note struck from the melody of the sky.

No. You haven't

'Yes I have. Nan says so.'

I lean forward to see if I can catch the haunting of his eye, the sad corner of his mouth. He tips his head further down.

'Mom found a sparrow on the floor yesterday morning.'

I remember the way the sparrows used to flock around the yard by the hundred, chirruping the ridge tiles, swooping to the weeds pushing their way through the edges of the concrete, stealing caterpillars and greenfly, scouring the rough surfaces with their beaks for breadcrumbs snapped from the tablecloth, and how they would sometimes fall from the sky like discarded pieces of memory, dislodged ideas.

Was it hurt?

Watching his shame I can sense how far apart we are. Far more than fifty years and a gulf of experience. Far more than a faulty memory. Less, but far more than a stranger, I realise how little he is learning to love himself, and I love him all the more for it now…

'It was flapping around and couldn't stand up. Mom picked it up and put it in there.'

He points to the milk-box on the wall beside the back door, a bit of stained rough ply big enough to hold four pints, a nailed-on sloping roof that lifts up to put the bottles in.

'Dad put a bit of wire in front so it couldn't get out until it was better. Mom let me give it some bread crumbs and some milk in a eggcup.'

Did it get better?

'No…'

And that was your fault?

He looks up at me then as if I won't believe him unless I can see the way it has marked his face, realigned the directness of his gaze, held shut some as yet unopened flower,

'Nan says it was. Me and Mick…'

Wiggy?

I see immediately Mick's plump-faced smile beaming out from under a blue and grey school cap.

'…we were going round the yard on our scooters, pretending to be fire engines like the one that came to see to the chimney. We were shouting and dinging like bells and Nan came out and told us to be quiet.'

And were you?

'For a minute, then we forgot. Nan came out and said we were making so much noise that if we kept doing it, we'd kill the sparrow that was trying to get better. We'd frighten it to death.'

Were you quiet then?

'For a minute, then we forgot. Nan came out again and sent Mick home, so I played on my own and when I went to feed it this morning it was dead.'

What did your mom say?

'She didn't say anything. She wrapped it in a bit of cloth from her sewing machine and put it in the bin when she thought I wasn't looking.'

What did Nan say?

Remembering now full and well the waspish stupidity that had often slipped from those unthinking lips.

'I told you so.'

He turns away from me to study the milk-box on the wall, as if trying to see the bird still there, still resting, still outside of this bitter memory, then turns back.

'Do you still like me, mester?'

Always, and it wasn't your fault

'Is it alright though… to remember things like that… even when you're not sure?'

Yes. For a minute. And then forget

He hesitates a moment, and searches my face for I can't remember what, some kind of brand or secret sign of truth that only small boys know how to access.

Tell me some of your big ideas

'Well...' he says. He rotates his shoulders independently in a circular motion I'd quite forgotten, '...me and Mick are going to build a rocket ship.'

That's brave

'Mom says it's daft.'

What does your dad say?

'He says if I can make it work he'll give me the money to do it, but it won't cost much.'

Why?

He looks around the yard and at the bin I'm sat on,

'Me and Mick reckon that if we took four bins and fastened them all together on top of each other and put a pointed end on, it would be big enough, 'cept dad says it might take six if Wiggy's going, so we'll have to pinch some from the yard next door.'

So how does it work?

'In the Library there's a book and there's this rocket engine that looks like a cannon but it's firing all the time and if we put one of them in the bottom bin that should do it. Mick and me are saving up our fireworks this year to try it out. I copied the picture. I'm going to ask dad to get me some pipe from work.'

Sounds like a good idea to me

'Yeah, but it got me into trouble again.'

I laugh sympathetically, remembering the apprehension that fills this small but questing soul twisting his feet in the yard, knowing that he will always feel the weight of other eyes depressing his shoulder.

How did you manage that?

'I told my teacher. She caught me drawing it when I should have been listening. She told my mom.'

What did mom say?

'She wanted to know where I got it from, this talk about rocket ships and space. I said that things like thoughts didn't have to come from anywhere, not like people. You can make them up from bits of things. Like making up a rhyme. They're things you can have on your own and they're nobody else's. That's what I think.'

He shuffles up onto the bin next to mine, his eyes searching me sideways, devouring the small logo on my tee-shirt.

'Is that true, mester?'

Never more so than now, Billy

I know that will be too cryptic for him, but I also know that he will remember the particular shape of this verbal jigsaw piece.

He reaches a slow, tentative finger across the gap between us. I watch it crawl cross fifty years and a billion freed ergs of energy to point unerringly at the Jacquard logo on my breast.

He continues, absorbed by the stitching, almost detached from the words he is speaking.

'Teacher told Mom I shouldn't be thinking about things that can never happen. I should be doing my spelling instead. But that's too easy,' His face colours slightly, 'I can always do that. Teacher says nobody can ever go to space so why bother to think about it.'

What do you think?

He slowly retracts his hand and drops them both into his lap, head down in thought, trying hard to put the words together. At that moment, I want more than anything else in the world to just put my arms around him and hold on tightly. To let him know things that I dare not say. But I never can.

'I think... that if we don't think about things... then they can *never* happen. Will it ever happen, mester?'

What?

'Space... and things.'

If you think about them, much, much more than that will happen. What would you like to do most?

'Go to space,' he says without hesitation, then adds, cautiously, 'and drive a train.'

Which first?

'Dunno,' he says, shrugging off a decision, 'Either.'

He looks across the yard away from me and I know, even without seeing, that I would recognise the screwed lip and the squint that means he is thinking over something he's seen or heard that has attached itself to a deeper thought pattern, one that rarely surfaces beyond a silent barrier of improbability in his head.

'That badge,' he says, 'The one on your shirt. What is it?'

Four bins... with a pointed end on the top

He whirls around to stare at me in disappointment, the originality of his original, haunting vision of space already beginning to crumble behind his eyes.

'So you thought about it, too.'

I didn't need to. It was enough that you did. You and a lot of other people

The sun threads itself through a cloud and his eyes catch up the light again.

'You mean... I'm not daft on my own?'

Never. There are lots of us. The ones that think they aren't daft are the ones that don't think. Then when they're in trouble or need something, they come looking for us

'To tell us off?'

I choke down hard on the laugh that rises, an inevitable bubble of hope that we share so intimately. I smile in restraint.

Only after we've saved them

'Saved them from what?' his look of puzzlement almost complete.

Dragons in caves

'That's my *best* secret!' he says, 'How do you know about that? Did mom tell you?'

No. I just know. But how do you know?

He slides off the bin lid to land back on his feet, takes two short steps away into the sunlight then spins on his heel,

'I listened outside the teacher's door. She told mom that all I ever painted was pictures of dragons coming out of caves. She said I must be scared of something. She said there might be something wrong with me. With that and the rocket ship as well. Do you think there's something wrong with me, mester?'

Absolutely. There's something terribly, wonderfully wrong with you

He stares at me with totally expressionless eyes but I can see they are a mask that conceals all the troubles and unapportioned blame that the world will ever present.

'What's wrong with me, mester? Do I need a Doctor?'

No. The Doctor needs you

He shrugs, despondent, dissatisfied with my response.

'Dunno what *I* can do.'

You can think, can't you?

'What about?'

Anything you like, that's your real best secret

'Such as?'

I look away for the first time since I've arrived. I don't want him to see the potential dishonesty behind my eyes, the fear of discovery, the knowledge that even at seven he is capable of discerning why I am here, the gift I've come to steal... the gift of that sheer unalloyed spike of inspiration, unsullied by too many fears and funereal doubts, hiding within the fragmentary sharps and flats of his belief that all things can sing.

I don't want him to share in the uncertainty of my position, or allow him to see that at some time in the future, even *he* will run out of ideas.

Want to hear my secret?

'Yes,' he says.

Come closer

His feet shift without hesitation, then pull back, innate common sense dropping into play. More than aware of his sense of preservation, I reach into my pocket and draw out a sea shell, identical to the one in his own hand moments earlier. I push it out of the shadow towards him, turning it slowly.

See the whorls in the shell? The way they are identical but getting smaller as we travel backwards in time to where the snail was born?

He takes out his and I place them carefully together on his upturned palm. Slowly, they meld into one. His face shines up at me, his eyes alight with answers already found, studied and discarded, chasing each other along the fever of his imagination. He snatches the shell and drops it in his pocket.

'How did you do that?'

I don't know. It shouldn't, but it always does it. Want to hear my secret?

He moves closer and I whisper into his ear the one Time Paradox I can't resolve.

He steps back suddenly, an exaggerated expression manifest across his face, infinitely recombining each left-over piece of aeroplane kit we have ever assembled without the instructions. He plunges his hands deep into both pockets, lost in thought for a moment, then draws out again the single shell. He holds it up to the sun so that the growth lines show dark against the pink light energy wavering through.

'What if… ?' he says.

Within that Darkness

Newton's Third Law of Motion…

…states that for every action there is an equal and opposite reaction. I think that this Law is incomplete. I have my own addition to it.

Allerton's Third-and-a-Half Law of Motion…

…states that for every action, there is also an equally unintended consequence.

Take the issue of the old Tate & Lyle Golden Syrup tin. It has a picture of a dead lion losing bodily fluids while flies buzz around it, and a Bible-quoting homily that reads…

'Out of the Strong came forth Sweetness.'

For years I thought that honey came from dead lions, possibly fermented by flies. Was that the consequence Tate & Lyle's action intended?

(Golden syrup is, coincidentally, a Newtonian Fluid with a density of approximately 1430 kg.m^3 at room temperature. A coincidence that, I believe, bears out my hypothesis. ;-))

Now we all remember the invasion of 1898, suitably documented by the renowned historian, H. G. Wells, and vividly reminded as we were by his later pseudo-relative, Orson, but we are privy to only one side of that particular argument.

What if, for the Martians, Allerton's Third-and-a-Half Law of Motion came into play…

(…and I STILL believe treacle comes from Lions…)

Within that Darkness

The silence of Darkness began to fail, the Avenue of The Dead becoming lit by the soft, fluorescent glow of a rising sun reflecting from the sides of the buildings. The crowd below settled, unusually hushed and quiet with the Light.

Sol-Eemin watched them from his first floor window, sorting the factions in his mind. Their numbers had grown intimidatingly since before first light, but he watched them now with a certain equanimity. He had reached out but there was nothing he could yet discern that would separate this crowd from the many others that had gathered there. He also knew that this could change in a moment.

A limousine slid silently through their midst and halted across the Avenue. A tall, slender human disembarked and turned to face the Great Hall beyond the avenue-wide steps that were its frontispiece. In his arms he cradled a small plexi-glass dome.

Sol-Eemin descended the steps to cross the plaza. Immediately the crowd saw him, full half of them turned. His assumptions had been correct. Raising their upper limbs they pointed towards him, their eyes emptied of all except contempt and their minds echoing one word…

'Betrayal…'

Inside the Great Hall of Antiquities, the Assembly was alive with speculation, yet their thoughts were unusually subdued by the sense of occasion. Above him, the translucent roof showed the remaining stars as hard, cold and uncompromising. Sol-Eemin hoped that by the end of this night, he too would no longer feel the need for compromise.

He observed silently from the dais as the human came to the table, set down his dome and withdrew the stasis clamps.

With the plexi-glass removed, Sol-Eemin moved forward and reverently lifted the tablet from its 500 year resting place.

Turning to the gathered assembly, he venerated this locked ancestral thought, then placed the tablet against his brow and began to project the patterns he found within…

'I am San-Ramin. I am a Searcher after Truth. And I am at once both lost and found. Allow me to describe my place.'

Sol-Eemin lowered the tablet. He stood for a moment in silence until he regained control of his lower limbs. He looked over to where the Earth Ambassador held station below and to one side of the altar and nodded in affirmation. This was indeed the mind of San-Ramin, venerated on this world for five centuries.

He raised the tablet once more and continued the projection. The thought faltered, then reached out and cloaked the Assembly like a shroud…

'As a child, I watched our world become as one without sunset. That Darkness which had once been ecliptic and a bringer of peace to our senses faded until all became continual clamour.

Since the first trick of life our minds have communicated. With the rising of the sun our minds become interleaved, each thought becoming a ripple passing through a million minds to return shaped, compromised and polished. In the time of darkness, our minds unlocked and we became as lost, single entities, with time for wonder at the things we had accomplished and time for reflection, pause, assimilation, and retreat from the touch of those million thoughts.

Throughout my youth I watched the sky above us, by our very industry, become a dense, enclosing sphere. The light of the sun spawned light-seeds across it, rooted and phosphorescent in a reddening arc that spanned the world.

Our Darkness was now infused with that same glow and so the unlocking, the time for reflection, became at first tentative then broken. Soon the pressure would begin, for beneath the weight of that sky, the heat of our industry began to circle back down upon itself.

It is fair to tell that in that search for perfection of self, that daylight mingling of consciousness, we became that machine which sees only with the coldest of logic; that sees only that which will accomplish. Later, upon reflection, we may each see the folly of our production, but who may say? How can we tell? For by Dark, we are only one island amongst many.

After many seasons, each more intolerable than the last, the idea of the accelerator was formed. Within a season its huge tubular bulk squatted around the equator reaching upwards until its tip broached the atmosphere and it was said that within its breech could be heard the whispering of the stars and the rumours of distant suns.

Our cylinders were to be accelerated by the simple device of evacuating the chamber then, with the aid of a small explosive impulse, allowing the terrible weight of our atmosphere to flood in, pushing them violently along the length of the accelerator. We were packed four to a cylinder, along with all that was thought necessary to ensure our survival.'

Sol-Eemin hesitated and with a little effort lowered the tablet. The Assembly swayed to the first touch of pain within the thought of San-Ramin as it stroked their minds with its hot, seeking tendrils. Sol-Eemin forced his attention back to the projector...

'And now, from within this velvet quiet in which I find myself, this other world seems cold and hostile and I find myself spent and for what, I cannot tell. I twitch a limb and the probe wavers uncertainly above my cabin. I am too feeble to assume the patterns required to engage the heat projector. Outside my viewplate, thought-nightmares jabber and point cruelly at my discomfort. I struggle to rise but the tripod is broken and twisted beneath the weight of the machine.'

Outside the Great Hall the crowd huddled together, diminished and trembling beneath the power of the mind of San-Ramin, relayed here across the plaza and from there to all corners of the planet...

'The shock of our arrival was both sudden and several as the cylinder skipped across the land as might a hard pebble until it came to rest upon its side. We lay in silence, recovering, as the ablation shield cooled and cracked until, slowly, we could begin to unscrew the lid.

Outside the cylinder was Darkness. A welcome, physical, hard, cold Darkness that enveloped our minds like a salve after our months long exposure to an unfettered sun. Following instructions, we quickly erected our shelter and changed the atmosphere within. We settled down then to wait for the dawn.

Above us, through the pale envelope of our shelter, we saw that the Darkness was relieved only by a scattering of stars. I remember at that time feeling the beginnings of a first true peace, but with the dawn came the Light and an end of those beginnings. A searing brightness filled one edge of the sky, moving slowly above a horizon so vast it seemed the hills rolled away for as far as my eye could see. With that Light came the first contact. In that instant, we shared all that we had discovered since the arrival of the first cylinder.

I have since become accustomed to the Light, though after the heat and pressure of our world, this place is cold beyond belief and the atmosphere both caustic and rare. There is a precipitation that burns our flesh, cratering the skin with unhealing sores. Life outside the cabins is at once vivid, vicious and intolerable.

We find that communication between us is enhanced, we think perhaps by the closer proximity of the sun. Our minds are linked with such clarity that we become alarmed by the ease with which we find ourselves engulfed. Within that clarity, we assemble our machines.'

Sol-Eemin paused to look out over the Assembly. On both sides there were those who despised this growing alliance of Mars and Earth as one of betrayal. They had been there for five hundred years, despite the advent of the selective projector. And now, this night, both he and they were about to be washed in truth, and one of them would drown. He raised the tablet and continued...

'We had prepared for the eventuality of finding life upon this world, despite its moist and prohibitive atmosphere, and our machines carried an offensive capability in which we had been but briefly trained. Some part of I/we was concerned at this capability in view of the purpose of our mission. Perhaps we may be found to have been guilty of over-reaction in its use, and no more. I allow you this judgement, but, in mitigation, after the attacks upon the first cylinders, fear became a strong and irresistible current within our mind. Subsequent attacks seem only to affirm the hostility of the indigenous life forms. They swarm upon us with their implements and we find their thought patterns intrusive and intolerable.'

Sol-Eemin reached out for the crowds reaction. Discounting the ordinary and the ambivalent, he found it in those who believed that war was inevitable. A growing depth of exultation and conviction. With an increasing concern for the future, he went on...

'We had little alternative but to tend to the task of clearing an area in which we could accomplish our mission. Fear and desperation drove us in that time. Fear for ourselves. Fear of failure, knowing that the deliverance of our race rested solely upon success. Fear of the native life forms. Their thought patterns are intrusive but completely alien and there is no common ground. We destroy them in the absence of time in which to reach an understanding. This world is hostile and our resources are meagre. Time is our enemy, and in the time we had we have wrought a holocaust. A holocaust drowned in our own fear, amplified by a sun of unusual proximity.

We had no choice. If a race expends its best energies in order that it might survive, and if that same race consumes its last resources so that its best thinkers can be delivered outside of that all-engulfing clamour so they may find peace within a Darkness in some other place, a place in which racial salvation may be sought in reflection and quiet consideration, then those minds are not free.

The means of our defeat are unclear. It may be an acceleration of age brought about by the power of the light, for I feel aged and weak. It may be a micro-organism to which we have little defence. I do not know and it is futile now to speculate.

Only these things are certain. My limbs are unsure and unsteady. My mind is filled with images of needless death. My body is filled with pain. Outside, it is mercifully Dark and my tormentors have fled. Our collective scream has subsided with the light, and I am quite alone.'

Sol-Eemin held the thought, listening to the crowd outside. From them came a sense of satisfying Darkness. He allowed it to envelope him, and from within that silent pool of drowning prejudice, he continued...

'I, San-Ramin, leave this record in the full and certain knowledge that I/we have failed, and in the faint hope that it may be found and accepted by those that assail us, should they one day aspire to intellect. The light within my cabin has faded and I know that the Darkness in which I find myself shall be my last. For within that Darkness comes the silence. Within that silence comes peace. Within that peace, you find me here, who once was lost.'

Sol-Eemin lowered the tablet from his brow.

A thought echoed from his extended projector.

'All Hail to Thee, San-Ramin.'

The Assembly stood in silent reverence. Sol-Eemin raised the tablet towards the sky. The thought was echoed by a million minds.

'All Hail!'

The Assembly lowered itself to the ground.

Sol-Eemin began the Litany.

'All Hail to Thee, Our Ancestors.

Whose passing rent the Sky...'

Outside the Grand Hall, Sol-Eemin turned to the Earth Ambassador.

'Thank you my friend. The return of this artifact can only serve to establish complete trust between our races.'

The Ambassador looked up to where the sun fell hard and short across the close horizon.

'San-Ramin should see this Light.'

Sol-Eemin made a comforting gesture.

'San-Ramin has his Darkness. In which one day we shall both share.'

The Ambassador smiled as they walked towards the enveloping City.

'Then together we may alleviate his sense of failure, my friend.'

'Indeed!' said Sol-Eemin, 'And toast his inadvertent success.'

He gripped the Ambassador's arm and led him from the Avenue of the Dead to where the streets now bustled in the Light.

'From my childhood I remember the stories,' he said, 'of the rushing of atmosphere along the accelerator. Of the tremendous whirlwind that developed about its breech that for many years no-one could approach and live. Of the way in which the balance of the upper layers was inverted and the phosphorescence fell like a golden rain about the land.'

He steered the Ambassador around a corner, his projector caught and guided by the thought-beacon of a nearby hotel.

He pulled the heavy cloak more firmly about him.

'And of the return of the Darkness.'

The Good Years

What can I say? Except that in many respects I *am* Jonathon Rowland. Okay, no electronic engineering degree, but I do share his passion for thermostat twiddling and for degrees Fahrenheit. (Not Celsius, they are an artificial construct sent by a Swedish astronomer to befuddle the rest of Europe.) Nor do I live in Stansted, or alone.

I am never sure why I have lived this far north all my life either, when sunshine beckons year-round in the lower latitudes. Perhaps it's because I like planes, but not airports.

I also like using mice in a story. My cat, Nell, likes them too. But where I write about them, she sucks them gently for a while until they give up, then brings them for my inspection. Usually around 3 a.m.

Dreams of Adulation? Don't we all have them? Jonathon wants to change the world and, in his hope for a warmer future, he reckons that if a Microwave speeds up molecular activity then, with enough power, running it backwards should be a cinch.

But he hadn't reckoned on the mice...

The Good Years

Jonathon Rowland craved warmth. Apart from this he was a quite unremarkable man. His career in electronic engineering had ranged from an early lack of promise across the whole gamut into redundancy, where, despite his most dire prediction, there was no equal or opposite reaction. Except for the fact that the office was now comfortably cooler and no-one fiddled with the thermostat.

Aged forty-three, he lived quietly alone on the ninth floor of an indistinguishable tower block in the town of Stansted, which is in itself quite indistinguishable, except for its Airport, the poor sister to Heathrow and Gatwick.

The descent path into the airport overlooked Jonathon's balcony, and he soon learned to recognise forty different aircraft by their undercarriage alone. The roar of the planes had become a fact of his life. In fact, they were a welcome diversion from his main occupation, which was to sit, wrapped in a blanket, nursing his pathological hatred of being cold.

Outside, the day was as pale as the walls of Jonathon's flat. The sun hung low in the pollution of a sullen sky with clouds building from the west. It would soon be summer, he knew, although at this latitude it wouldn't matter how long the clouds stayed away, there wasn't enough heat in that ghastly glowing orb to lift the outside temperature more than two or three degrees, and whilst that was better than not, it didn't make up for the long cold nights and the general air of depression about the place.

He sat, cocooned as usual in a blanket, in front of his computer and toyed idly with the mouse. He clicked on the icon that allowed the pointer to trail images of itself as it moved across the screen, then wove it around as might a child with a length of ribbon tied to a stick.

He stopped, thought for a while, then opened up a new screen and began to work.

Within three months the first box was complete. It was mostly unremarkable except for the sheet lead plating on three sides and the top. On the front was a small glass door and a set of control buttons stolen from the microwave that now lay disembowelled in a corner.

Jonathon tightened the final screw then closed the flat door behind him. He took the bus through the rain to a nearby pet store, returning later with a large white mouse that he named, after some reflection, Santa Fe.

He placed the mouse inside the box. Once inside, if his calculations proved correct, the mouse would be delayed in time by one tenth of a second, for every one tenth of a second of operation. He set the timer for thirty seconds and switched on, then watched with a bemused expression as the mouse, somewhat bemused itself, rotated with the turn-table.

At the end of thirty seconds the bell pinged and Jonathon withdrew the mouse. He placed it carefully on the table. It sat there a moment as if unsure of what was expected, then it began to move.

It took three cautious steps.

Behind it appeared a trail of connected snapshot images of itself, so that it resembled a small white concertina with whiskers at one end and a tail at the other. After thirty seconds the first images began to disappear, and the mouse shrank up to its new position on the table at the same speed at which it had walked.

Jonathon turned back to his computer.

The mouse, forgotten in Jonathon's haste for greater things, described a perfect arc in the air as it jumped from the table. It then drew a straight white line across the carpet as it ran towards the ruined microwave. Thirty seconds later, the line un-drew itself in the same direction, but by then Jonathon was working too hard to notice. If his deliberations proved correct, it should become possible to externalise, or even project the field.

Seasons passed, in which Jonathon was far too busy to give anything other than a cursory thought to the white trails that occasionally criss-crossed his carpet between the kitchen cupboard and the hole in the skirting board. He just stepped over them and continued to punch the keyboard.

Behind the skirting, over by the remains of the wrecked microwave, Santa Fe met Maria, a brown house mouse with a very willing nature. A few weeks later, new small trails began to appear, some of them tinged with brown.

Maria's best advantage was that when she wanted Santa Fe, she always knew where to find him. It didn't matter that he came in the first few moments, the thirty seconds it took for the rest of him to catch up was adequate compensation. Their family grew apace. The children inherited their fathers time delay and although Maria thought they were a little retarded for their age, she loved them dearly.

Jonathon was building a new box, much larger than the first. Totally absorbed, he never noticed as the carpet changed from its original blue with small pink flowers into a streaming white and fawn abstract.

Outside the flat, the weather retained its constant variation between lashing rain and a weak winter sun that never actually managed to wring out the puddles.

Inside, Jonathon huddled beneath two blankets, hating the cold more than ever and warming his hands against the soldering iron.

The box was nearing completion. A writhing mass of coils, looms, and solenoids, it hulked upon the table beneath the electronic equivalent of a permanent wave. Periodically, a mouse ran through it while Jonathon was working, linking it to the table with an elongated mouse rope. Some time later it would unravel and disappear across the floor towards the corner of the skirting behind the dissembled cooker, stereo, video and microwave.

When he surfaced in the damp, dreary mornings, the curtains would be festooned with mouse trails. The worktops and food cupboards had become a maze that only time could unravel. He would switch on the kettle and wait. After two mugs of sweet, tepid coffee he would cast a worried frown over the way in which some of the trails were taking longer to clear. A slice of pale, dry toast later he would shrug and switch on the soldering iron.

At the far end of the living-room was a door that led out onto a south facing balcony. It was just large enough for a second-hand deck chair, an insipid pot plant, Jonathon …and the box.

He stepped out onto the balcony. It was 11:15a.m. and for once the day was dry without looking menacing. The sun was close to its highest ebb above the bank of radar dishes to the south.

Jonathon retraced his steps into the living room as the dust on the balcony swirled in a sudden jet-wash. The sky shuddered as ten about-to-be-tortured tyres screamed past the window.

He looked up and smiled.

DC10. On Goodyears. High profile.

Jonathon took a screwdriver from his tool roll, wrapped it in a cloth along with a large pair of insulated pliers and sneaked down into the basement. Working quickly and quietly he cross-linked all the electricity supplies into the single meter connected to his flat.

As he stepped back out of the lift he noticed that his door was slightly ajar and that there were mouse trails across the landing towards the flat next door where his neighbour, a somewhat unremarkable young woman, kept a tomcat by the name of Geronimo.

He hurried inside and found that he couldn't close the door for the trail. He nipped through into the living room to put down the tools where he noticed at once that the mice had dislodged the coil connections from the tertiary disassembler unit to which they had been taped. It wouldn't take him long to trace back through the wiring and re- colour-code that section. He looked at his watch. Fifteen minutes to midday. There was still time.

Jonathon struggled the completed unit out through the door and onto the balcony. Once there, he ripped the insipid plant from its pot and balanced the box carefully on top of the upturned earthenware.

He had spent part of the last evening forcing four separate mains power cables into one set of connections and now he snaked the wires back across the living room, disconnected the standard lamp his wife had left behind and pushed home the plug. Out on the balcony, the box set up a gentle hum.

Jonathon tuned it until the aperture at the front faced the sun. He adjusted the four lead plates through which the time delay beam would be focused on it, then took his place in the deck chair. Pulling the blanket around him, he reached over and pressed the switch.

Nothing happened.

Down below in the basement, the tortured mains wires began to glow with the strain of supplying the box. Four streets away a sub-station tripped out first one subsidiary circuit and then another in the effort to divert extra power to the demand.

Across the river, the power turbines slowed as current was transferred from the National Grid to keep pace with the growing drain. Like slowly falling dominos the grids began to shut down, first one sector then another, to keep pace.

Amongst the first to overheat were Heathrow and Gatwick.

Jonathon had been sitting quietly on the balcony, the box humming gently beside him. He wasn't alarmed or dismayed when nothing seemed to happen after the switch was pressed, he had expected that, and after all, anything worth having was worth waiting for, and this was going to take Time.

Within twenty minutes the sullen red glow of the sun began to take on a more ovoid, elongated appearance and Jonathon found he could roll the blanket down from his chest onto his knees. He opened a button on his shirt in anticipation and waited.

After two hours the sun had become a deep golden band of spilled egg yolk oozing low across a quarter of its winter arc. Jonathon's shirt was now open to the waist and perspiration rimed the fringes of his hair. He closed his eyes and dozed off in the warmth of another season.

Nine floors below him, people returning to work from lunch suddenly decided not to and went home to enjoy the unusually early burst of summer, thinking that it couldn't last.

Out over Europe the sudden increase in temperature kicked a high-pressure weather front into action. It pushed out northwards to where the colder air descending from Siberia nudged it sideways and east towards Asia. It compressed itself into a heavy cloudbank covering most of eastern Russia then tipped down towards the Med. From there, the rapidly expanding air over Africa nudged it northwards back into Europe, where it began to spin.

The young woman in the flat next to Jonathon's hadn't noticed the dappled beige mouse sheltering under the edge of her doorstep as she returned.

Geronimo was much sharper.

The mouse hurtled off and back through the still open doorway into Jonathon's flat like a bullet train. Geronimo, startled, sat back in amazement. The front of the mouse, whiskers and all, had shot off like a rocket, yet still here, right in front of where he now sat in shock, was the rear end. He put out a tentative paw. The mouse's tail was stretched out straight and level as if it was ready to run. Geronimo couldn't quite make sense of it.

Eventually he decided that when a cat is presented with at least twenty feet of prime beige mouse it has to begin somewhere and this seemed like as good a place as any to start. His mouth began to fill with saliva. He narrowed his eyes, bared his teeth, and pounced.

His jaw hit the floor with a dull thunk as the mouse trail shrank over the threshold and disappeared inside. With more than a few reservations, Geronimo followed the Santa Fe trail.

Out on the balcony, Jonathon was dreaming. Dreaming of Medals of Honour, Nobel prizes, high profile lifestyles. After all, the effects appeared to be cumulative and permanent, given the evidence of the mice. His machine would revolutionise the Northern Hemisphere. From now on there would be summer plants, flowers, fruit and grain crops all winter, all basking in unashamedly luxurious sunshine.

He would become known as 'The Man Who Filled the Sky'.

His remaining years would be mostly good years! Summers would always be sub-tropical. Palms, Hibiscus, golden shimmering beaches with shimmering golden women; mornings so glorious he wouldn't be able to sleep for anticipation of the coming day's warmth and an absence of aches and blankets.

His balcony would riot with fresh fruits, grapevines would strew across the living-room ceiling and the gentle drone of year round bees would buzz beside him like the box.

He would sleep naked and shame the neighbours.

After just a few minutes more...

Air Control had a bit of a flap on. The only pocket of good weather in the Northern Hemisphere was over the Home Counties. One by one, Leeds/Bradford, Manchester and Birmingham airports had all succumbed to a gathering storm driving like a huge Catherine wheel over Britain and Northern Europe, with London at its epicentre. The few southern airports were still marginal but the weather was closing in fast. At this stage they weren't too worried, after all, within the London radius there were three airports with good visibility and excellent facilities to cope with the extra traffic.

That was before Heathrow and Gatwick went out.

Geronimo pushed the door wider and looked cautiously around. Everywhere he looked there were mouse trails. They covered almost every inch of carpet, ran up the curtains, over the worktops and under the various bits of discarded electrical equipment in the corner. He prodded one. It zipped out from under his paw like an elastic band. He sniffed at another and began to wonder if he had died and gone to cat heaven, for under his nose were several hundred feet of prime mouse sausage.

He stalked along a row of several trails that intertwined their way across the carpet to the shell of a ravaged cooker. He lifted the door with an inquisitive paw. Twenty or more mouse trails exploded out from below the grill and shot straight for the open door that led onto the balcony. They ran at full tilt beneath Jonathon's deck chair, up and through the protected centre of the box and back through the still open door into the living room with Geronimo in hot pursuit. The heads of the trails disappeared beneath a pile of electronic debris.

The cat stopped, studied the trails where they passed out of the door onto the balcony and decided that when confronted with this much food, it didn't matter where one began. He took hold of the fattest trail with arrow-sharp teeth, and pulled.

Jonathon was revelling in the cheers of the crowd. In fact, the crowd were cheering so loudly in the ear of his dreams that he didn't hear the box slip along the tightened mouse trail and onto the floor. As it slid onto its back beside the deck chair, the directional shields that had been taped into place fell away.

Still dreaming, he listened in his head as the roar shuddered the sky. Their shout was like a great wind passing. Again and again they roared until he thought their throats would be torn in adulation of him, and their voices wrapped him like a cooling breeze.

In the street below, the sound of horns began to rise as the traffic gridlocked to a standstill.

Without opening his eyes, Jonathon reached down and pulled up the blanket. Warm again, he returned to the roar and fanfare of the crowd in his dreams.

Overhead, the sky began to fill with the trails of aeroplane tyres.

Mostly Goodyears.

High profile.

Fearful Symmetry

I read somewhere a long time ago that Poetry and Science Fiction are almost mutually exclusive. I never believed it totally, although I will subscribe that the difference between Poetry and *Futuristic* Fiction may well be that one describes emotions that predate us, and in which we can all share historically, and that the other pre-empts us with as-yet-unrealised situations for which we may have little or no emotional experience or reserve on which to draw.

That said, there had to be a way. So I left it on the backburner for a while until one evening I ended up in a discussion with poets about the different forms that poetic language could (or should) conform to. I am certainly of the opinion that all real Poetry should have scansion, preferably a rhyming scheme of sorts, and preferably not a really dogmatic and obvious one, and all else beside that is Prose, in one form or another.

It became clear to me during the debate that this linguistic Origami that the 'poets' were espousing, may not be the only thing that Poetry was capable of folding. What about Time and Space? Why the Haiku not? How dangerous can it be?

Fearful Symmetry

Beyond the Starliner window a pastoral scene slid gracefully by. Beside a lake, beneath the trees, a host of golden daffodils danced their blaring trumpets.

Sheep, continuous as the stars that shine and twinkle on the Milky Way, dotted the green as if they were daisies cast upon a distant lawn. Emily turned away from the lonely clouds that wandered high o'er vales and hills and groaned.

'Not another Wordsworth.'

Grandfather leaned over to pat her knee.

'It'll be alright. You'll see.'

Emily assumed the air of bored indifference that, at twelve years old, she felt befitted that of a seasoned space traveller.

Grandfather returned to the scene outside the window. A smile settling reverently across the warmth of his face.

Watching his reflection in the glass, Emily wondered if he'd always been that old. There was something so solid about him, the way he dressed so darkly somber, that she guessed he always had. She picked up the Vidisk he'd bought her at the spaceport and began to read.

The Wug on the seat beside her clicked happily and rhythmically, it's pleasure sensors weaving expertly amongst Emily's gently moving fingers. After a while she put down the Vidisk and began to fidget.

'I want to see the Poet.'

Grandfather turned away from the window and re-focused his eyes.

'He'll be busy right now.'

Emily tugged at the ribbon on her pigtail.

'I only want to look at him.'

The Wug, sensing her displeasure, wound its sensors around her fingers. The rhythm of its clicking increased to match that of her heartbeat then slowed, bringing her pulse under control, easing away the frustration.

'Just to see...' she said.

She returned her attention to the screen of the Vidisk. Turning it over in her hand, she saw that it had been written for 'the discerning twelve year old' and pushed it disgustedly from her. The Wug clicked rapidly for a few seconds then slowed.

'Just to see...' said Emily, wistfully.

Grandfather smiled and nodded, reminding himself once more that the Wug, a harmless, mood-modulating creature recently discovered on Graves 5, was the best investment he had ever made.

Emily lifted her hand unsteadily from the seat. The Wug clung tightly to her, pulsing it's displeasure into her fingers, making her aware of the danger she was putting it in. Emily felt it thrill along her arm, felt it drill into the centre of her cortex.

Suddenly the world was bright and fierce and fickle. Springing like a red, red rose, it blossomed with thorns and dangers unseen. She bounced the Wug once for spite, as if she were about to drop it, then lowered it safely back to the seat. As the Wug clicked back into it's steady rhythm, her senses withdrew into a state of rest and the world felt safe again.

'I want to see the Poet,' she said.

'Oh, Look,' said Grandfather, pointing out the window, 'There's another sheep.'

The Poet lay still and silent in his cot. Despite the wires, Emily thought there was a degree of serenity about his face that made him look far younger than his years. The temperature gauge inside his container showed a hundred degrees lower than the rest of the ship. She pressed her face against the glass canopy and drew faint wavy lines in the condensation.

Grandfather tugged gently on the sleeve of the gingham dress Emily had tried desperately to leave behind at the Station.

'Come away, now. Let him rest.'

Emily stared through the glass, fascinated by the shock of frosted black hair that crowned the Poet's head. It curled evocatively against his ears where the red velvet wrapped him in it's electric cocoon; the stiff white collar around his neck perfectly in keeping with the beautifully laid frock coat.

'Doesn't look like a Wordsworth,' she said, 'More like a 'Poe'.'

Grandfather frowned, 'We'll have none of that. This is a family cruise.'

'I know,' said Emily, the disappointment evident in her voice.

After the first ten sheep and several hosts of golden daffodils she'd found herself wishing that she'd been old enough to travel the Pentameter Line, with their 'Hughes' and 'Eliot' ships, though she'd always thought cats too remote and fussy. Or maybe a 'Blake'. Her big brother had said that the tiger's eyes burned right through your soul. Emily didn't believe him. He was always making things up just to frighten her.

Even though she had learned in Primary about the Iambic Drive, and understood the way the deliberate constraint of rhyme folded the fabric of space like one of those Station concertina postcards, Emily still found it hard to look out of the window and accept that the sheep were not sheep, but stars drifting by at super-light speed, and that the green was not grass but the Poet's interpretation of the collapsed darkness between.

Grandfather looked out of the single window in the Poet's cabin and tugged her sleeve once more.

'Come on,' he said, 'Let's take our seats. I think the sun is about to come out from behind that great thunderhead over there. The daffodils should look particularly fine today.'

Emily shrugged his hand away. The Wug, attached to her fingers began to click rapidly, sending calming pulses through her nervous system that she fought hard to ignore.

'I want to stay.'

She stared down into the Poet's casket. A wistful smile floated lonely as a cloud across her face.

'I think he's handsome.'

Grandfather glanced around the cabin. It was empty of all harm apart from the sealed casket containing the suspended body of the Poet.

'Alright,' he said as he left, 'Five minutes. No more.'

Emily ignored him, her fingers already searching around the glass.

Five minutes later, Emily returned to her seat. She checked the scene outside of the window and smiled briefly before picking up the Vidisk.

Grandfather was fascinated. Emily had never seen his old face so alive with interest.

Beyond the glass the sun was now low and powerful and red and the daffodils blared themselves into death with a sullen, yellow fire like a brass band at the Gates of Hell. They streaked the window as the Starliner slid through, their pollen etching into the glass.

Inside the Poet's container, the Wug was dying from the cold. It had sleeked its fur along its length until it seemed no more than a wee, timorous beastie. Finding no comfort in itself it attached to the Poet's fingers, twining its sensor array around and in between, digging deep for the warmth it hoped to find within. Steadily, it began to pulse its distress.

In the far distance beyond the window, a sheep disappeared. Something orange took its place. It moved on to the next sheep and that too disappeared. As it moved from sheep to sheep, the orange thing grew larger and more graceful.

Grandfather stared, horrified now, as locusts devoured the green. They left behind only the blackness upon which the thing walked. It strode across the Starfield, aglow from within by the fires of many suns.

All sheep consumed, it stood for a moment, its fearful symmetry framed by the window. Emily looked up into its tiger-eyes and felt their hunger burn right through her soul. It watched her for a moment in silent reproach ...then stepped through the glass.

Future Imperfect

It is a long time since I first met Harry. Too long, really, but when I started to look for suitable inclusions for this book, I found him again, still making his way along the Park path and marching triumphantly into a future beyond his comprehension.

If there is a moral to this story, it is that we are never sure of what is really happening, even when it's under our noses, and that we can never be sure of who or what a person is, even when we think we know them so well.

Harry's present is none too comfortable and he finds himself subjected to enormous indignity and oppression, but his life is turned around in a single moment of Epiphany. Will you find yours? And when you do will the accompanying music be Fugue, Operatic, or Triumphant… like Harry's…

Future Imperfect

Harry's brown gabardine coat bent the fresh breeze around him, keeping him safe and warm beneath the trilby hat that Mr Gill insisted on cramming upon his head. Carried up the lazy 'S's of the town side of the park by his slow ponderous gait, he reached the place where the wind kept its year-round grip on the escarpment. At the top he stopped to listen. The hedgerow along the ridge carried the flusters of small nesting birds and Harry held still a moment, memorising their songs. Beside the path, the daffodils and croci were little more than dank brown husks. Harry knew their scent was blown away a month gone along with the last of the snow, but soon there would be other colours, other scents and this morning the air had a newness about it, whilst seeming almost afraid to let go of the chill.

From where he stood, the ground sloped gently away towards the Hostel in the field beyond the edge of the park. The path meandered back and forth across the hillside, disappearing behind an occasional bush, reappearing in small clearings with lath-back seats and mesh litter bins.

There were few people, though Harry avoided even these whenever he could. When he couldn't, he nodded politely the way Mr Gill had shown him and hurried on his way. Harry listened to the sound of the wind across his ears, a soft susurration.

'Sssshhhhrrrrr,' he said, until the sound of his own voice in his ears balanced exactly that of the wind. At that, Harry smiled, and set off down the path towards the hostel. He took the first turn, marking strict time by the soles of his heavily scuffed boots as he negotiated the small hairpin. At the first clearing he stopped and sat for a moment on the empty seat, his fingers tapping time on the hard laths. He stared down the hill towards the hostel, towards its bleak, slab sides and the corner with the window where he knew Mr Gill would be sat watching, always watching.

Harry waited. He knew Mr Gill would wait, then when Harry moved he would be up and attend to his business until such time as he looked and Harry was stopped again. Harry imagined he could see him sat behind the window at the desk. Harry hated the desk. He reached up and touched the hateful hat. Mr Gill couldn't ever let him free, Harry knew that. That's why he made him wear the hat, so that he wouldn't ever forget. He waited a moment or two longer, knowing Mr Gill would be fidgeting by now, clearing the desktop in case he returned late. At first Harry had cried out, but now, if he was late, he just laid there, white, sullen and shaking until Mr Gill was finished. At the thought, Harry stood up, passed through the sparse rhododendron bushes with their bright young leaves and into the next clearing.

There were two people on this seat, a man and a young woman. Harry knew he shouldn't stop at this one, he should keep moving until he found the next empty seat before stopping again. If Mr Gill saw that he had stopped near other people then Harry would be punished when he got back, late or early. He placed one hand on the hat and nodded then made to hurry away.

As he turned, the young woman spoke. Two sounds. Two notes so pure and clear that Harry stopped and looked straight at her. She made the sound again. Harry smiled and repeated the two notes, exact in timbre, pitch and tone. The woman looked sharply at her companion. He turned to Harry and spoke two more notes. They were the same two notes but in a much lower key. Harry repeated them faultlessly, his face breaking into a wide grin. He chimed the notes repeatedly, willing the people to speak. This was the first music he had heard since Mr Gill had stolen his radio. All he had was that which was left inside his head, making its endless concert loop in Harry's musically perfect memory.

By some ancient quirk of the brain, Harry was unable to perceive even the simplest of words, but he understood music in a way that only he could comprehend and now, at the sound of the woman's voice, Harry had understood. It had been a simple greeting. The man's had been the same but, somehow, more questioning. The woman spoke again to her companion. She opened her soft mouth and Harry listened spellbound to the beautiful glissando of her voice, knowing unmistakably that he was in there, and that she had spoken about him.

Down below in the hostel, Mr Gill cleared his desk and watched from the window. High on a shelf in the office was Harry's radio. The single red-rimmed eye of its dial glared down at him. Mr Gill shuddered. It wasn't a fit thing for an idiot. He remembered Harry's face the day he had taken it away, then smiled. Harry had remained sullen ever since. He stood up to the window as, far across the park, Harry, instantly identifiable by the hat, sat down on the grass to listen. Mr Gill reached for his coat.

Harry smiled broadly at the girl on the seat. She herself remained silent, studying him in return. Harry turned his grin towards the man. The man seemed absorbed in thought, one hand determinedly stroking his chin. He leaned towards the girl and spoke again, the notes falling faultlessly through Harry's broken brain, assembling themselves quite effortlessly into speech patterns that for once in his life he could understand.

'I don't recognise him.'

Harry wondered at this. Had he seen these people before?

'There are so many of us now, scattered through time,' said the girl.

Harry struggled with the communication. So many Who? So many What? Harry knew that the Hostel was filled with people. He didn't know all of them but they all knew him. How could these people not know him, couldn't they see the hat?

The girl turned to Harry, the bell-like tones of her voice tripping along an ethereal scale.

'Who are you?' she asked.

Harry's grin widened. These people didn't know. They didn't know about the hat! Didn't know what it meant. Slowly, he realised that, with these people, he could be whatever, no, whoever he wanted to be. A laugh gurgled sudden in his open mouth. He threw back his head and from deep within his throat came the sound of string instruments being plucked in unison.

'Da da da dum dum, dum dum,' sang Harry, rising to his feet, 'Dum dum dum, dum dum dum....'

He skipped across the path in time with the music.

'I'm not certain,' said the man, observing Harry closely, 'but perhaps an Earlier?'

The girl shrugged.

'More likely a Later. He recognises our speech patterns, perhaps as archaic, while his seem strangely adrift, somehow without logic. More like… that's it… more like a construct, like… poetry, even.'

By now, Harry was stalking an invisible wolf through long grass and dark woods, an imaginary rope coiled about his shoulder. The couple listened intently.

After a while, the girl began to chuckle.

'I have it!' she said. 'His name is Peter, and it's his story. It's simplistic, childlike even. It must be allegorical.'

The man watched as Harry prowled the bushes, wrestled with things wild and unimaginable behind the seat.

'Yes,' he said, 'it's simple, but you have only the half of it, don't you see?.'

Harry was hiding now, peering at them through the mesh of the basket.

'He has to be a Later,' continued the man, 'But much, much Later than any we've encountered before. The childishness, the simplicity, you understand? That's for us, that's for our benefit.'

The girl watched Harry in awe.

'To think that one day we shall have such freedom,' she said, 'Such capability of expression!'

The man nodded silently, then looked up.

'Someone's coming. Quickly! Show him the pager. He may know how to fix it!'

Harry followed the man's gaze and watched as the stick-like figure of Mr Gill turned the gate at the bottom of the hill and began the slow steady climb towards them.

The girl held out her hand, palm up. Within her palm was what looked to Harry like a thick, round, button. He felt along the edges of his coat. No, it wasn't his. He disregarded the button and pointed towards the place where Mr Gill had momentarily disappeared behind a bush. From his throat came the low growling sound of many, menacing, lupine horns.

The man found himself gripping the laths of the seat, his knuckles glowing white and crimson against the dark wood. The girl sat back sharply. Fear and confusion crossed her face as the threat within Harry's voice infiltrated to the very depth of her being. She shuddered involuntarily, crying out at the approach of such violence. The button fell from her hand to the gravel where it winked briefly at Harry, like a small, pale, sunlight. Silent for a moment, he picked it up.

The girl was the first to recover.

'Please!' she begged, 'Please! Be quiet. Say nothing!'

Harry's next rumble died in his throat. The girl and the man sat, dismayed and panting. Turning the button over in his hand, Harry could see that it was dull where it could be shiny, like the dial on his radio had been. He turned it around. There were small figures on it and a thin red line but no sound came from it when he aligned one with the other.

The girl held out her hand towards him. Harry clutched the button instinctively to his chest.

'No, no,' she said, allowing him a cautious smile, 'I just want to touch you. I want to touch the future, to see what it feels like.'

Harry didn't know about futures, but her smile was warm and her voice held no threat. He reached out his hand and slowly, their fingertips touched. Her arm jerked back as though shocked. Harry looked disturbed. The girl raised her palm towards him,

'No, no,' she said, her voice gentle and soothing, 'It's alright.' She turned to the man, 'There is so much! There is too much! We could never learn... not even if we spent our lives...'

Harry looked from one to the other as they stared at him in awe. He smiled and nodded, just the way Mr Gill had said. Mr Gill! Harry jumped up and searched the parkside until his eyes found Mr Gill, halfway up the path, breath steaming quickly in the pale spring air. Harry found his own breath catching in his throat as his heart beat faster and faster. In fear and frustration he began to rub the button fiercely on his coat. Up and down, up and down, in time with his heartbeat, the dull oxide layer abrading from the contacts, faster and faster. It began to grow warm, then hot, until, as Harry pressed, it seemed to sing in his hand. The man touched his sleeve, Harry startled like a buck.

'Please,' said the man, 'be calm. Tell us, we'll help you. Is this man a threat? A threat to all of us? What shall we do? What would you have us do with him?'

Harry leapt into the middle of the path where he could see Mr Gill climbing towards them. He shook the fist holding the button into the sky, his fingers surely crushing the contacts. He threw back his head and from his throat roared the siege of Moscow, and suddenly it was winter, and just as suddenly there were cannons and cymbals flashing and crashing. The man and the girl strove to breathe, their chests crushed beneath the weight of death and destruction surrounding them, filling the air as if the world were suddenly turned in upon them and itself. Harry subsided to a rumble as Mr Gill disappeared again behind a bush. He waited, anticipating, seeming to know just where and just when Mr Gill would re-appear. At the precise moment, Harry shook his fist once more into the sky,

'Boom, Boom!' he roared, 'Bu bu bu bu, bu bu bu bu, bu bu bu Boom Boom!'

'Boom, Boom!' said a pale green patch of cloud in the sky.

The man and the girl exchanged frightened glances. She clung to the man's arm.

'What if...?' she said.

'No, they wouldn't,' said the man, 'They must have seen... must have heard!'

'Boom, Boom?' said Harry, curiously, to the sky.

'Boom, Boom!' said the sky. Harry opened his fist to look at the button that was now cooling within his palm. It winked unevenly at him, then stopped. He closed his fist around it and pushed it deep into a pocket. The girl, startled, made as if to grab for it. The man held her back.

'Stop. It's too late. We can only hope they have seen ...have enough sense.'

She clung to him as a soft green glow fell gently around their shoulders. Their outline faded like the old grass beside the path. Then she smiled when she saw that no similar glow enveloped Harry.

'Goodbye,' she said, 'and thank you. We wish you well.'

Harry looked to where Mr Gill was stalking up the path towards him, scant yards away. He held out his hands towards the girl, begging, pleading. Tears welled deep in his eyes. He opened his mouth and from it leapt harps, immediately drowned by cello, scythed through by violin. The girl shook violently, her eyes closing. The man shrank back. Harry fell silent once more. Within that silence the girls face became pale and drawn. Slowly she opened her eyes to Harry. Her smile was fainter now and Harry thought that he could see the shape of the seat behind them showing through, like stars through mist.

'I'm sorry,' she said, 'But you cannot come with us. We are not ready for you. You have so much power we would have no defence against it. You would walk through our lives like a god.'

Mr Gill caught up to where Harry stood with his arms outstretched and grabbed roughly at his sleeve. Harry ignored him completely.

'Idiot!' shouted Mr Gill, pummelling away at Harry's shoulder, 'Idiot! Come away!'

Harry had ears only for the girls voice. Tears streamed down his face as he watched her fade, remembering, remembering her voice as it diminished.

'Far worse,' she had said, 'You would become a god amongst us, robbing us of our aspirations. You would be The Future Now! And that should never be.'

And with that she had gone.

Mr Gill took hold of Harry's sleeve and pulled him around. Harry looked down at him, a curious expression on his face.

'Boom, Boom!' said Harry, loudly.

Mr Gill fell backwards onto the grass, his face a mask of fear and confusion. Harry took out the ruined button, examined it almost carelessly.

'Boom, Boom?' said Harry, to the sky.

The sky remained silent.

'Boom, Boom!' said Harry, to no-one in particular, and threw the button into the mesh basket. Turning, he took off the hat and crammed it down upon Mr Gill's head. He spun on one heel and set off down the hill towards the Hostel. Mr Gill found himself jerked to his feet as if by an imaginary rope, and was dragged, flailing, down the path behind Harry.

They had barely gone ten paces before the full, rich, sound of seventy six trombones filled the air.

Bruv

What is the true value of money? Whether in a pre- or post-apocalyptic world? Does it's concept change with our circumstance? What does it buy? Material things? Comfort?

But what if there's nothing to buy and you can only dream. Will it buy a dream? And would you really want that dream if you found you could buy it?

Perhaps in a post-apocalyptic world, the ability to move and keep on moving is the only thing that has any value. Can money buy that? Or is it what anchors us in our modern day perception of currency where a huge mortgage can be a desirable display of wealth and success.

Suppose that, on one day, the way to your dream sits gleaming in the palm of your hand, reflecting in your eyes with relentless sunlight and promise. What would the animal buried deep inside of you buy then?

Your dream or your freedom?

Bruv

I take a deep breath, wheeze a little from the dust.

'Take this road,' I say.

Harich bounds around me, skippin' over the coon-tail straps of his pack.

'It's all part of it, part of that whole damn 'moth-candling' thing. You get on and it sort of draws you along.'

Harich grunts, slides off into the edge and kicks dirt into the hot dry air. The desert waits out there, wide, silent, watching. I spit the dirt from my mouth.

'F' Chris' sake Harich!'

Harich falls back to the middle of the road. He drops to all fours, wide squat nose truffling up the faded centre line.

He laughs, 'Harich Snufflepig!'

I kick his rear.

'Get up, F' Chris' sake!'

For a moment he slaps along beside me, hunched away from an expected blow, great feet plating the hot tarmac. I reach out and he shrinks away. I pat his head, stroke the downy nape of his neck, brush a little dust from the mat of hair down the length of his spine. He turns. He smiles.

'Bruv.'

Don't matter how many times I tell him I ain't his brother. Don't matter anyways. Might as well be. I was a loner 'til they banged me up, put me in with Harich. Seems like another life, well, some way ago now.

Harich walks behind me, doggin' my steps like a one o'clock shadow. I feel his hot breath, hotter even than the day's breath, on the back of my neck. I stop. He stops.

'Harich!'

'Bruv Bruv...'

It comes from somewhere close behind my ear. I turn. He smiles, fangs gleaming in the desert dust of his face. He tips back his head and laughs deep down primeval inside, deeper than his open throat, somewhere else way down in the past where it has something animal-boned about it. Some days he scares the shit out of me but I'll never let it show.

I kick him in the shin.

'Harich, don't do that!'

His face falls, closing the vast cavern of his mouth. Inside him the thunder rumbles like it does across the desert dark mornings. I wait for the lightning that will surely one day come. The thunder passes. It 'solves away into his quiet murmur, passin' slowly, eyes cast.

'Bruv ?'

I ignore him and walk on. Harich stands his ground muttering. The tension fades behind me with the distance. The wind falls. I listen. Behind me the faint slap, slap of feet begins.

'It's like I said Harich...'

...back over my shoulder, words falling like dust on the wind...

'...like this road. Comin' from nowhere goin' someplace. Just like us. An' nothin' seems as if it can stop it.'

I wait, silent in the fall of wind. The slap, slap comes and then is torn away across the shrub and brush, tumblin' out of earshot.

'Like I said. Like walkin' a destiny. Like walkin' the lines on your hand. Knew a woman once said she could read a man like a book just by the lines on his hand. Said my life would take many paths. Hell, I could've told her that! Been moochin' since I can't remember. You too I guess. Eh? Bruv?'

Harich slaps up beside me, panting. I turn without stopping.

Harich looks up, 'Bruv?'

I smile. He ducks. Does a kind of half skip.

'OK,' I say, 'I'm Bruv.'

The road picks up about two miles ahead and tricks a cleft around two bluffs sticking up like piss-proud boners. Town's the other side. I know. I ain't never seen it but I heard Tell an' Tellin's all we have left an' so it has to be right.

A Teller has to be kinda careful. It ain't no job for no liar, leastways, not for long. Last Teller we met was five days gone. Two more behind since we escaped and those spent guessin'. Life don't leave no room anymore for guessin'.

We paid the Teller an old scrub hen Harich ran down flocking with a pack of ro-birds. They took no notice of him, kept peckin' away and liftin' stones and searching in the dust and the rust for somethin' who knows what.

Harich wanted to take him with us. The Teller, that is. Parcelled o'course. I said no, Teller was there when we needed him an' if we all did that then there wouldn't be no Tellers no more and life would be all about guessin' an' I guess we'd probably all end up probably dead ...I guess.

Harich had smiled at that, a large serpent-like smile, fangs white on red. He'd looked at me with wide expectant eyes.

'No,' I'd said.

Harich bounds along, sometimes in front, sometimes dropping off behind before chasin' up, kicking dust-devil swirls off the heat-haze blacktop. The packs are lighter now. It's two days since we left the beach an' the shrub-hens we caught were gettin' lean and hardly worth the slicin'. We have enough until we hit Town and then maybe it's anythin' we can steal. We ain't got nothin' else left since we paid Teller.

Harich stops dead in front of me. I rattle his heels with the toe of my moccasin.

'Get on, Harich.'

He doesn't move. He bends down and I fall over him and down we go all legs and packs spillin' out an' the dust gettin' into everywhere and my eyes stingin' from Harich's arm across my face like a pole-axe.

'F' Chris' sake, Harich.'

The sun pulls my eyelids closed against the swelling. My britches rip across the knee-backs. Harich puts out his hand. Grips my arm. The lightning draws back.

'Bruv!'

Harich points to a small round hole in the faded blacktop. I can see something in the bottom. It's dull where the dust sits on it like the years on my face when I look in a pool. I blow the dust off, my face pressed close to the road. The sun gleams back up at me like a beacon.

'Dig it out, Harich.'

Harich levers the small round disk off the road with talons grimed with dust and pitch. Hands it to me.

'Bruv?'

I pick up a handful of dust and rub the disc between my fingers, polishing the surface. I spit dry-mouthed into a paste and spin the rim on the edge of my sleeve. A man's face gleams up at me. On the other side an eagle grips like death on a flag.

Harich shuffles, jostling for a better look. I push him away.

'It's a coin.' I spin it in the bright heat, 'I hear tell there was lots of 'em. They say a man could get whatsoever he wanted with one of these, Bruv.'

I close my fist and feel the coin round and hard inside my hand.

'Whatsoever he wanted…' I pause, then draw a rich mans breath.

'Bruv? Hold?' says Harich.

I hesitate, toss the coin once more up towards the sun and watch it fall bright and spinning back into my hand. I clutch it tightly.

'Okay,' I say.

Harich snatches it from my hand, his fingernails drawing furrows across the skin. He hunkers down in the road and examines the coin, turning it over and over in his fingers.

He points to the eagle, shakes his hands up into the sky, fingers like dark, thick feathers splayed on the desert wind.

'Ro-Bird.'

'No,' I say, 'Well, Hell, maybe yes.'

He turns the coin over.

'Bruv!' he says, stroking the face gently with a talon.

I laugh.

'Yeah. Big Bruv.'

Harich roars with laughter, mouth wide and fearless.

'Big Bruv! Big Bruv!'

He leaps around, pushing the coin up to my face where it gleams in the blackness of his talons.

'Put it away, Harich.'

He slips the coin into the little pouch he's made inside the 'coons head on the top of his pack.

'Careful Bruv,' I say, 'Don't go losin' it now. That's a dream, Bruv. A real dream.'

Harich gambols on ahead. I know it's safe.

A mile up the road a Snufflepig crosses the highway, snatching up the remains of a wreck with its wide distended maw, its great bulk blotting out the twin bluffs, the attendant flock of ro-birds sweeping like a black wind across the road, peckin' an' turnin' the dust around the space where the wreck had been, smellin' metal with magnetic noses, siftin' with plastic beaks and wings. We slow our pace and watch it drift towards the horizon, the Grindworms in its belly chainsawing their noise across the sand behind it.

'Come on, Harich.' He picks up the pace. A half skip. A stumble. A smile, an' then he's off up the road apiece, scuffing the blacktop with wide, splayed toes, looking for coins.

'Hey Bruv,' I shout, 'Ro-birds got 'em all?'

He smiles and pats the 'coons head. I laugh at the look on his face.

'Ok. Not all, Bruv.'

In an hour we top the rise where the road tricks around the cleft and then falls down, down aways into Town. I pull up to the shade of a bluff, drop the pack and put my back against the quiet stone. Harich is off down the road, seeing nothin', hearing nothin', still looking for the glint of gold in the blacktop.

'Hey.' The echo comes back at me from the bluff across the way. Harich looks around, puzzled. He can't see me in the shade.

'Hey!'

He gallops back up the road then turns and sees me. He dives across and jumps me, fangs out clean and white, talons raking in lookin' for throat and skin to tear. He stops, grinning, an inch from my face.

'Hey Bruv!' he says.

I pat his head and the lightning goes away. He points down the road.

'Town, Bruv.'

His talons sink deep into the flesh of my arm, pulling me irresistibly to my feet. I grab his ear with my free hand and twist.

'Let go, Harich!'

He lowers me back into the dust.

'Sorry, Bruv.'

'I should think so. Set down quiet. We wait.'

'Wait what why, Bruv?'

I pat the dust beside me.

'For dark. Set down and be quiet, I want to think.'

Harich sets the pack down beside me in the shade of the tall slender rock, his feet and legs stretching out into the road. He picks up the 'coons head pouch and begins to croon to it, looking deep into its empty eye sockets as if there were something that should be there, something as animal as himself that was missing and torn from it with a knife. One of them things no matter how fast you moved you couldn't never seem to put your finger on, nor never see which way it went.

I seen that light go out myself and never thought to wonder before I met Harich. Perhaps I'm too far and gone from the animal in me. Perhaps that's why Harich and me kind of fit together, like he's a part of me that I'm missing and wouldn't never have known it if it weren't for him.

I think on the coin. I heard tell of coins, never expected to see one though. Strikes me it ain't big enough to do all the things a man heard that it could do. I wonder if a coin was maybe just for one thing. Not like a shrub-hen, not like a 'coon that can be cut up and sliced to buy maybe two, three things at once.

I remember how it felt in my hand. Hard, hot from the blacktop. There ain't no way I could share it. It may be a man had to have one coin for each and every thing he wanted.

Perhaps before the ro-birds found 'em, coins were just littered about like dreams waiting for a man to pick 'em up. Somehow it don't seem fair that we should have only the one dream between us. Perhaps Harich doesn't dream.

Harich grunts, shifting beside me, never taking his eyes from the 'coons dead and empty sockets.

I wipe the sweat from my face.

'Do you dream?' I ask him, hoping that the answer will be 'What Dream, Bruv?'

Harich places the 'coons head gently on the top of his pack and wraps his long arms around hunched knees. He bends his head between them. The answer comes muffled and low as if even shifting the dust were sacred, his face buried and gone from sight.

'Woman,' he says.

Shit. I should've known he'd say that. That was how he'd ended up in the slammer. I was figuring on maybe hot water from a long tub to soak away the taste of holding pens and deserts …and a little of that cactus juice they have in Towns, the kind that makes your head fall apart and then puts it back together in a different kind of way and you can still feel the nails in the mornin' but hell, it's fun while it lasts.

Harich takes the coin from out of the pouch, licks it, holds it up and looks at me with the lightnin' flashin' way back in his eyes.

'Woman,' he says.

I pull out the knife, a flensing blade hooked like a beak.

'Shave first,' I say.

After dark we pick up the packs and set off toward the fires and the smoke from the Town. Harich is scraped naked and trembling in the thin desert air. The Town's a mile or more off and spans a ridge so it's hard to tell where the fires leave off and the stars begin with their flickerin' an' all. The desert's black as sky and the hot wind's whistled back to some hole in the ground from where it'll leap out again tomorrow an' suckin' with the heat to take a mans last drop of fluid down to his bones.

I guess I been lucky that way, with Harich. Harich can smell water a mile away. Old water, new water. He can tell it right off. When he gets close he can even smell water buried right there under the sand, sat waiting away from the heat for a man to dig. Some days we just set and pushed our hands into the quiet cold to soak the parch from our skin.

For once Harich pads along silently beside me, the soft bustle of his breathing the only sound in the dark, deep, desert night. Off to sunset, lightning cannons back up to the sky, flashing the underneath of the clouds. I see the answer in Harichs' eye. I count the seconds...four...five...a soft rumble sounds deep in Harichs' chest. His mind's away, thinking, dreamin'.

I feel him dark and animal beside me in the night. He smells of hot dust and somethin' else. Then I realise it's the smell of my own fear, driftin' up and fillin' my nostrils now the wind's died. Fear of Harich, fear of Town, fear of being banged up and fear of tomorrow. Maybe that's how a man stays alive. Maybe he's just too afraid to die.

We hit the first shacks barely out of the desert with wide spaces between 'em full of nothin' but the night. Harich and me, we drift in and out like black smoke in a tar pit.

We keep out of the light. Harich ain't afraid of fire, I'm afraid to let 'em see him. The way he looks, it ain't pretty.

I park him in an empty hut about a third of the way in. Three sides are stood but the fourth bangs across the front tippin' the roof edge up like it's pointin' at the stars. In the corner away from the fires it's pitch. Harich melts into the shadows. I take the 'coon pouch from his pack and tip it out into my hand. The coin takes the firelight before I slip it inside the hollow of my cheek and push it down against my lower jaw, safe from trick-johns and slitters. Harich's hand comes out the shadow like it's cut off at the wrist, like it's floatin' in the dark, and grabs the band of my pants.

'Bruv?'

'Yeah, Bruv. I won't be long.'

I pat the hand where it grips like an eagle on a flag.

'You gotta stay here. Promise me you'll stay here.'

He doesn't speak. His breath whiffles in and out rapidly and then settles like it does when he's thinkin'.

'Ok, Bruv.'

I know he'll stay. He thought about it. It ain't like one of those things he does when he says OK right away and you just know his head's full of skips and jumps and this and that and turn your back and he's off somewhere stumblin' an' snufflin'.

'Bruv?'

His voice seems deeper comin' in from the dark. I like the dark. It settles Harich.

'Woman, Bruv?'

Oh hell. I thought I'd got him off that kick.

'No, Bruv. Food. Eats. Cactus juice.'

There is a faint rumble. Back there in the dark, I think I see… no … just sparks in my head. I slip away.

'Back soon, Bruv.'

Town is full of shadows half-pressed against the huts and trailing people as they cross the open-spaced firelight. I walk further in, courtin' the dark like a lover. There is a growing noise, like Grindworms, like rocks chasin' each other down a scree and I look up expectin' a Snufflepig then remember they're programmed to skip the Townships an' then remember again that the sound is only people goin' about the things that people do in Towns and how quickly the desert helps you to forget.

I catch the arm of a man who streams out of the firelight pushing his shadow long and slanted across the ground. He stops and looks at me, his eyes like the 'coons empty sockets in the dark. He's so close I can feel him breathing, long, deep and steady. His arm hangs limp in my grasp. He turns his head and nods in the direction of a large shanty, piled two, maybe three storeys high, just the other side of the fire.

'Over there,' he says.

His voice is dead like the night, like the spaces between the huts, like an echo in the desert.

'What's over there?'

'Whatever you need. Whatever you got. It's all the same. All ends up right over there.'

His arm slides through my fingers. He breaks away into the night and is gone.

I move around an edge of the firelight until I'm stood outside the shanty. The walls are some kind of wavy tin and where it doesn't fit right the gaps are ablaze with light. A large tube sticks out through the roof and I see heat and sparks pourin' out into the night. Around the back I hear the steady putter of an alcohol generator, almost lost against the rumble of voices from inside. I find the door and slip through the sackcloth drape into the heat and the light and the noise.

In the centre of the room a huge tube comes down out of the ceiling and beneath it there's a brick hearth with flames shootin' up sparks and dirt. The tube glows red hot for about five feet before it disappears into the ceiling. The heat from it's like the noon-day sun. The bottom of the tube is turned out into a rim and a kid is flippin' coon steaks and pushing root vegetables around on the glowing metal. The smell knots my empty stomach.

Nobody looks at me. I stand for a minute an' let the heat suck the desert night out of my bones. Across the room there's a counter with bottles of cactus juice and what looks like clear water except I know it's wood alcohol …and a man never sees more'n his first drink of that.

The room is full of people, mostly men, talkin' and not lookin' an' mindin' never more than small amounts of each others business. A woman grabs my arm from behind.

'What can I get you?'

My throat catches when I look at her. Faded as a centre line. Thirty five. Lost looking. Filthy. Some teeth, mostly round the front. Not pretty. Never was.

My voice comes back like a shadow in the heat and light.

'Cactus juice.'

'What you got?' she says.

'What do I need?'

'Somethin'. Anythin'.'

'Well, I got somethin'.'

'What you got?' she says.

'Nothin', I guess.'

'Then that's what you're gettin'.'

'Hold on,' I say, 'What about this?'

I retrieve the coin with my tongue from the inside of my cheek and poke its milled edge wet and glistening between my teeth. Just a glimmer so she can see I ain't kiddin'.

Her eyes grow big and round like bloodshot moons.

She slaps her hand to my mouth and growls.

'For Christ's sake put that away. You want to get yourself skinned?'

She takes my hand. Hers feels hard and horny and not like I'd sort of expected.

'Come with me,' she says.

She takes me to a corner. We duck through a drape and suddenly we're climbing stairs in total darkness and I look through a chink in the tin sheets and there are the stars right out over the desert away from the glow of the fires. We duck through another and into a room that's lit so bright it hurts my eyes. The tube runs up through this one too. The heat is unbearable to an outsider like myself. A tall, lean man sits behind a small desk up against the far wall. His clothes are sharper and better cut and more like the old style than any I've seen in a while. Behind him, a curtain is drawn across a window against the night. Two other men lounge on chairs at either side of the drape we came through. The tall man folds a book shut and puts it beneath the desk out of sight. He looks up without smiling.

'Hello, Manny.'

The woman speaks quietly but her hand trembles in mine.

'Sorry, Mr Dee, but I thought you'd better see this right away.'

The man continues, unsmiling.

'See what, Manny?'

The woman nudges me, pushing me towards the desk.

'Show him.'

I turn around. The men by the door are sittin' upright now. The one on the right is gettin' the balls of his feet beneath him. His weight shiftin' almost unnoticeably.

I wear my brightest smile.

'Show him what?'

I feel a knife point sharp against my ribs. I look down. It's hers.

'Show him. Show him the coin.'

The man behind the desk starts to rise.

'A coin?'

'Looks like gold, too,' says the woman, 'Kind of hard to tell in the firelight though.'

I retrieve the coin and spit it into my hand. I hold it up high, the spread eagle flashing in the heat and the light.

'You mean this?'

For an instant their eyes are gripped like the flag. I twist, turn, my hand comes away from hers, free, as the coin slips back into my cheek and the knife comes away from her hand and into mine as if she'd pushed it there.

The man from the right lunges across, hands reaching for my throat. I fade around the tube into the waiting arms of Mr Dee. I elbow him good and hard, drop, turn out of his grip and swing him by one arm around and back into the tube. His clothes melt and stick to the metal. I see the back of his hair catch fire.

I wonder where the third man is, then I see him sprawled into the corner with the woman called Manny, blood flowing dark between them with Manny shuffling hard to get out from under. The first man comes back around. He stops to pull Dee, burning, from the tube. I hit the draped window feet first, fall ten feet then hit, bounce, slide and roll from the tin roof of the shanty into the black dust by the generator. Dee's screams echo in my ears. I watch him topple forwards from the same window, clothes blazing like a falling star. His first bounce showers sparks back up into the night sky. He hits the floor beside me and lays still. The fire sputters out. A hand snakes into my hair and drags me flailin' backwards into the shadows.

Bastard!' she says, 'Stupid, stupid Bastard!'

I realise then that my breathin' has stopped, and I fall winded into the dark edge of the shanty. Manny pulls a loose tin sheet across in front of us and lays tight against me. Her cheek is up against my lips and nose. She smells like a week-dead 'coon. Pretty soon there's a commotion and a lot of voices and nothing, it seems, from the man on the ground.

The voices go away, draggin' somethin' heavy. After a while, Manny slides the sheet away and pulls me off into the dark away from the people millin' at the front of the shanty. We head out into the desert then skirt back around to where I left Harich. I approach the hut from the shadows, keepin' Manny behind me.

'Harich?'

'F' Chris'sakes!' says Manny, 'What kind of a name's that?'

'Don't matter none,' I say, 'We're brothers.'

I hear the whiffle of Harich's wakin' breath.

'Bruv?'

'Yeah.'

I hear him sniff the dead air.

'Woman, Bruv?'

Oh Hell.

'Yeah. I guess.'

I pull Manny into the dark of the shelter.

'Say hello to Harich.'

She moves closer to the shadow in the corner of the hut, pushes her hands slowly into the night-space.

'It's ok,' I say, 'You can touch him.'

Her hand draws back quickly.

'Kind of stubbly,' she says.

Harich sits quiet, lets her touch him again.

'Kind of strange,' she says.

'Nah, that's just Harich,' I say, 'He's different, is all.'

She looks up at me, eyes lit by a star no more than a passin' spark.

'Thought he was your brother?'

'Well, yeah. Sort of…'

'He's a mutant! I ain't touchin' no mutant!'

I grab her wrists until she calms down.

'He ain't no mutant. Doc in the pen said he was a throwback, and that's what makes him special. That's Harich.'

'You're sure he ain't no mutant?'

'Doc says he's…' I pause to get my mouth around the words, 'Nee-and-earth-all-man.'

'Sounds kind of homely,' she says.

'Well, I guess by daylight you could call him that.'

Harich shuffles around in the dark. His breath whiffles in and out rapidly like he's tryin' to say somethin'. Like he does when he knows it's goin' to make me mad. His hand reaches out of the shadow and touches Manny gently on the shoulder.

She sits bolt upright.

His voice breaks out of the dark.

'Woman, Bruv?'

'Hell no! Not for nothin'!' she says, 'An' I ain't 'Woman'. The name's Manny.'

I lift Harich's hand from her shoulder. It disappears back into the dark.

'What the Hell kind of a name's that?'

Manny edges away from the dark in case the hand comes back.

'Was Mr Dee. He gave it me. Said it's like short for Mannequin. Said I was a store bought dummy.'

'Never heard of it.'

'It's in the book. The one under his desk. Called it a dickshunary. Said it's full of the old words, like the ones that pulled us down. An' he said it helped him remember how it must have been once and how they could push us up again if only more of us remembered.'

'Kind of like the coin, maybe?'

'I used to rook the 'johns while they were asleep, go through their packs an' all. Dee said if I could find him a coin ...showed me one in a picture all gold-lookin' and shiny ...said it would buy me out of here.'

I watch her face fall haggard in the firelight.

'Where would you go?' I say.

'Don' know,' she says, 'Twenty years ago it might have mattered. Was just a dream, but boy you killed it good.'

'Then why 'd you help me?'

She looks up and the shadows hide the lines in her face. I see a dark patch on the rough tunic near her left shoulder.

'Don' know,' she says, 'Maybe I thought you was just too stupid to die. As if there ain't enough stupidity in the world.'

I laugh softly.

'An' I thought I was just too afraid.'

'You ain't afraid to be stupid,' she says.

I put out my hand to touch the dark patch on her tunic. She paws away my hand.

'Got nicked in all the fun. Tain't much. Can I see the coin?'

Her eyes go big and round in the flickerin' firelight as I pull the coin from out my cheek. I hold it up and turn it slowly, watchin' the light and dark play over it.

'Can I hold it?' she says.

'Not 'less you can get us some food. An' maybe a little of that Cactus Juice.'

She gives me a look like I was a new disease and then she's off duckin' the light across the compound. Harich sits quiet. The tension is comin' in waves from out the dark.

'Soon, Bruv. I say.

Manny returns half-dragging an old beat-up pack.

'They're all outside the Canteen stomping Dee into the dust. Guess he weren't ever'bodys favourite. I went in at the back. It was easy.'

The patch on her tunic looks bigger but the food smells wonderful. I pull cooked meat out the pack and push it into the shadow. Harich takes it gently from my fingers and for a while we sit quiet and eat.

Manny reaches into the pack for a bottle of wood alcohol. She pulls up her tunic. Her breast hangs low, and dark with blood. She washes it from the bottle. Her skin is pale and the lines on her face etch deep as the alcohol seeps into the wound. It don't look much, but you never know what the blade's pushed inside. She drops the tunic and wipes her hands on the hem.

'Let me see the coin.'

I slip it from the pouch on Harich's pack and hold it out to her.

'Here.'

She presses it to her lips, presses it cool against her forehead.

'It ain't every day you get to hold your dream,' she says.

I sit quiet for a time as she sways gently on her knees. Her eyes are tight shut, lips workin', mouth saying silent things into the firelight. I hear Harich breathing softly behind her.

'What about Harich's dream?' I say.

'No,' she says, eyes still tight shut.

'You done worse things.'

Her eyes spring open, she lowers the coin into her other hand, grips it tightly.

'How you know what I done?'

The tin feels cold and hard against my back.

'I been round 'most as long as you. You done what we all done. What had to be done.'

Her eyes close like two black holes in the sculpture of her face.

'Alright.'

I touch her forehead gently.

'Thanks.'

She brushes my hand away and looks kind of scared, lines tightenin' in her face, 'Only if I can carry the coin.'

I shrug, 'What 'bout when we leave?'

Her eyes catch with the fire, 'You think I'm stayin'? Might s'well die right now.'

'Ok.'

The coin'll be safe with her. Out in the desert it won't mean a thing and she'll die without Harich to find water. She slips the coin inside her cheek.

Harich's hand reaches out and touches her gently. His fingers curl around her waist from behind.

She stiffens.

'It's ok,' I say, 'While ever I'm here.'

She leans forward into the light, spreadin' her fingers in the dust.

Harich draws her slowly back into the shadows until only her face remains. I hear the rustle of her tunic and Harich's breath lift like the morning wind.

Her eyes snap wide, her mouth a cavern in the glow of her face.

She cries out. It's a sad, animal kind of sound. Like you might hear way off in the night when you know somethin's been took. I put my hand out towards her. She looks at me and I see, way off in the back of her eyes, that same animal lightnin'. I back off into a corner of the hut and the only things that exist are the sounds of Harich takin' and the crackle of firelight on her face.

She throws up her head.

Her throat rattles like a ro-birds wings and in that instant I see a chink of light disappear down her throat.

We take her with us.

Two days later we get the coin back. Two more after that and we leave Manny sittin' in a wreck by the road burnin' up with fever and shakin' and the blood flowin' all down the front of her tunic with no sign of stoppin'.

There's a smell about her that we all know. Harich looks up at me, eyes wide.

'No,' I say.

We've not gone far when a Snufflepig drifts by and snatches her up, wreck and all, grindworms chainsawing away on the wind. A ro-bird comes close, flits over us then returns to the flock.

'Hell, Harich.'

He stops, waits for me to catch up, doesn't look back.

'She got her dream. She's well out of there.'

The soft slap, slap of bare feet falls in beside me.

'And you got yours,' I say.

I fold my fingers tight around the bright, hard coin.

'Guess there's just mine left now.'

Harich grunts.

'Bruv?'

'Don't I got one too, Harich?'

He stops beside me.

'What dream, Bruv?'

'Hell, Harich, if I told you that somebody might go an' make it happen. An' then it won't be a dream no more. Might as well give up right now. Get on out there. Find me some water. You smell awesome.'

He trots out into the edge of the desert, head turnin' this way an' that, searchin' for somethin' only he knows how it smells. I unfold my fingers slowly and the coin falls into the soft dust.

I listen for the sound of dreams crashing.

Nothing.

The desert bends the wind around me, searchin' out the water in my soul. I pick up my pace.

'Hey, Harich. Wait for me.'

I never look back.

Pestware

Back in my early days of computing, after the Sinclair ZX80 and the glorious 16k Spectrum, each of them tangled with tape cassettes that either would or wouldn't load depending, it seemed, on the 'R' in the month, I bought an Olivetti 286 (I still have it! And it still works!)

Pre Windows, this new and advanced level of computing brought with it 'Microsoft Works', a trio of programmes (not Apps, please…) that gave me a spreadsheet and a database that I never acquired the skill for. But the word processor revolutionised my writing. (For better or for worse is your call.)

Following that momentous change, we had, in rapid succession, Email and the Internet. Through Compuserve's Forums I made the acquaintance of many other writers, some of whom I am still in touch with.

One of the first things I found on there was 'Testware'. This was 'Shareware' software on a 3.5" floppy disc posted out to you for a modest sum plus postage. There were some weird and wonderful programmes in their catalogue; one for instance that dialled any of my telephone numbers by the click of a screen icon, others that created Fractals, given that you might have to wait half a year for the programme to finish.

There were even programmes that would find you quotations from religious tracts.

I felt that the concept was truly amazing, and began to wonder what else they might supply on a trial (or 'Beta' as it's known today) basis.

This story is old, sexist, sarcastic, dry of wit and generally weird, just like me…

Pestware

I was waiting for my cassock to dry. I threw it over a radiator and picked up a copy of The Ecclesiastical Times from the common room table.

The ad read:

Testware

Menu Driven Computer Shareware.

This months special!

#3287:BIBLE COMPANION

Designed to aid and assist your pursuit for perfection (In a strictly Biblical Sense)

Requires: 64K Ram, 40Mb Hard Drive space
Registration fee: None.
Basic Companion + Full Instructions

£25.00p.
(Access/Visa/Paypal)

Please allow one week for delivery within the U.K.
(Guaranteed for one year, chapter and verse!)

About 6 a.m. there was a knock at the door.

On the other side was an olive-skinned woman wearing nothing more than a shift. In her arm was a bushel and a light shone dimly from under it. I was never that lucky, so I gave up there and then and slid back between the sheets.

She must have followed me in.

I raised a battered eyelid.

In the dim glow that followed her in from the corridor she looked about five nine in her leather criss-cross open sandals and the shift hung loose from pointed places below her chin and on down to her ankles. Her hair was dark and half way down her back in ringlets. Around her wrist was a plastic tag. It read:

#3287: Bible Companion (Salome Model.3)

I looked her up and down. The room was mostly dark and she still hadn't found where the light was coming from.

'OK,' I said, 'It's under the bushel. Either get into bed or I'm going back to sleep.'

She stopped fumbling and began doing things with her hair. I turned over.

I don't know what I'd expected for £25.00, no Registration fee and only 64K of Ram.

She shrugged off the shift, leaned over and breathed, 'Oh Ye of Little Faith!' (Matthew 14:31) in my ear.

The days sort of blurred after that. We went through the Book. Genesis was good while it lasted but each time we came she'd shout a different name until it felt like we'd begat the crowd at Wembley and after a while it began to pale and I started to want to do really weird things like, get out of bed, or eat or something.

She complained.

I said, 'Know ye not that a little leaven leaveneth the whole lump?' (1 Corinthians: 5.6)

She took me in hand, 'I am the resurrection, and the life.' (St. John 11.25)

I had to agree. I squirmed to the edge of the bed and wagged away through to the kitchen.

'Thou art absent in body, but present in spirit,' she sang. (1 Corinthians 5:3)

I switched on the toaster, called back, 'Feed my Sheep!' (John 21:16)

Exodus was wild. Every time she came, I went. One time she got up to make breakfast and left the wings on the locusts and God knows what we were drinking.

After three weeks I sent her back under guarantee. I attached a note to say that our systems had become incompatible, my hard drive was beginning to resemble a three and a half floppy and there wasn't a format left that we hadn't tried somewhere along the line.

Three weeks after that I got the statement from Next. How can one woman wear so many veils at once, and on one credit card? They said if I didn't pay, they'd have my head on a platter. Now that's what I call a Switch.

Miriam came by special shipment. And went back the same way. Who needs all that water?

Mary should have been a feast, but I was passed over for the guy who came to fix the bed. He said he'd like to join her.
Well, we all have our own cross to bear.

The Company were pretty good.
They said they were set up to deal with the occasional devoutly awkward sod and that didn't mean that I was any less of a Christian, oh no, God Forbid, but I was working my way down their list from Alpha and pretty soon I'd be at Omega and all they'd have left to offer would be no. 99: Wedding Night Simulation, where I took my own hand in marriage.

The next one arrived in a plain brown wrapper. I checked the label on her wrist before thumbing through the Good Book to find her chapter. There was nothing. She sat there looking smug with her legs crossed and a cigarette burning slowly between her fingers with the smoke drifting languidly up through her tousled blonde hair. Her smile was painting lip gloss on the rim of a glass of strong white cider.

She looked up and laughed when I said she was a fraud. She pulled the hem of her skirt down an inch. It sprang back three.

'Sorry, love,' I said, closing the Book, 'I can't find a Tracey anywhere.'

'It's the wrong Book, John,' she said.

'Wrong Book? Wrong Book?' I thought, what's wrong with this woman, there is only ONE Book!.

She hooked her seven inch heels into the bar of the stool, tugged at the hem of her blouse and sort of poked and shifted things around in the top.

'No, John,' she said, 'Wrong version. That's King James. I'm New Essex.'

She unbuttoned her blouse and pulled my face against her chest. The world blanked out.

'I am he that liveth, and was dead!' I mumbled, (Jude 1:18), 'And the name's Mark.'

She blew hot breath through the short hairs at the back of my neck before undoing my trousers.

'How great a matter a little fire kindleth!' (James 3:5) she said.

I realised then that perhaps I wasn't cut out for the cloth.

Tracey was the best yet. After two weeks I had less spine than the Book, the fridge was empty and she'd drunk the entire contents of my wallet.

I had to go out. I needed money and food and I wanted to send an extra ten quid to the boys at Testware. She told me not to worry, it went something like…

'It's easy for a rich man to pass through the arse of a camel and if I catch you giving anyone the eye I'll get the right needle and while you're out, a six-pack of Diamond White would be Heaven.' (Tracey 60:9)

I was getting angry, 'You see me as having nothing,' I said, turning out my empty pockets, '…yet possessed of all things!' (Corinthians 6:10)

'Ah well,' she said, picking up her clothes, 'Just make sure my reference reads: 'This woman was full of good works.' (Romans 9:36)

I beat her to the door,

'Hang about,' I said, 'There's a guy down the road whose car hasn't moved for a week. I'll look it over, there might be a few quid in it.'

She pushed me aside, then hesitated,

'Why tarry the wheels of this Chariot?' (Judges 5:28, Tottenham Rd. Magistrates Court, £10 fine.)

'His driving is like the driving of Jehu;' I said, 'for he driveth furiously!' (Old Bailey 9:15, Last Wednesday)

She laughed like a woman scorned. What the hell, she was furious.

'14th. Commandment,' she said, 'New Essex; Thou shalt not nick the wheels off thy mate's Cortina.' (Stansted 6, Southend United 2)

'Thou shalt not get caught!' I said, (Devil 1, God nil.)

She waltzed back into the room. I caught her by the wrist and spun her around. The tag came off in my hand. On the inside it read:

Possessedware

Demon Driven Shareware

Succubus, Mark 2.

At least this time they'd got my name right! For a moment I didn't know what to think. Maybe it was a Clerical error.

'Behold,' I said, 'The half was not told me!' (Kings 10:7)

'How long halt ye between two opinions?' she asked. (Kings 18:21)

Her smile was all-knowing, all-seeing, all woman.

I need the money, I said (Nat West. -200:Red)

'Hurry up then,' she said, 'and come back to bed, where the worm dieth not and the fire is not quenched!'(Mark 9:44)

I had to laugh, for God loveth a cheerful giver, (Corinthians 9:7), and at least she'd stopped calling me John.

'Give it a rest,' I said, 'I need to stay me with flagons, comfort me with apples, for I am sick of love.' (Solomon 2:5), 'And I could murder a beef sandwich.' (Marks & Spencers, Aisle 3: Rack 4)

She leered at me across the bed, 'How can he get wisdom, whose talk is of Bullocks?' (Ecclesiasticus 38:25)

And I'd thought I was making sense.

'And by the way,' she said, 'did you know I had 3 sisters? If you ring them they'll join us. They're on 020 666...'

'Hold on,' I said, as she shredded my jeans, 'Armageddon all I can cope with!'

'Then gird up thy loins as a man!' she said, (Job 38:3 unfinished)

'...I want my Apocalypse... NOW!'

Titles in the CYBERMOUSE BOOKS range>

Our books are carefully selected, edited and published to bring you the finest reading experience whether on Kindle or in paperback.

'The Fox & The Fish' by Bill Allerton, ISBN: 978-0-9548373-2-7

Beset from all sides by Lovers, Coffins, Friends and Tinkers, Julius McEarly is forced to confront the greatest enemy of them all… his past. Set in Ireland, The Fox & The Fish carries a gentle but adult humour in a winsome, engaging storyline interspersed by moments of supremely funny 'codology'.

'We're in Ireland, and never far at all from the likes of Flann O'Brien, Joyce, Milligan, etc.. Casually very clever, so puzzling and allusive and fast that it makes the world more interesting when you stop. It gave me weird dreams; it is a weird dream.'
Rony Robinson (Author, Playwright and Sony Award winning BBC Radio presenter)

'Firelight on Dark Water' by Bill Allerton ISBN: 978-0-9930424-4-7
All of Life is in here. Seasons, Change, Wishes, Cookery, Sex, Death and Obsession, Guns, Trees and Bananas… even second hand Japanese brake parts…

'If you wish to be surprised and delighted by the change of direction presented in each story, then this is the book for you…'

'A Day for Tigers' by Bill Allerton ISBN: 978-0-9930424-3-0

A life-long love affair with Sci-Fi and Fantasy comics led to the collection of Bill Allerton's short SF stories into this 'Weird and Wonderful' edition.

In this book I have tried to recreate the sense of discovery that I felt when I first encountered SF, so… if like me you are still seven at heart, and also, like me, you are still in love with the Golden Age of Science Fiction and Fantasy, that you find that heart again within these pages.

'Warrior Girl' by Pauline Chandler ISBN: 978-0-9930424-0-9

Suppose, for just one moment, that your best friend has embarked on a path of faith and self-belief that will lead you into murder, intrigue, bloodshed and battles in which your own hands will not remain clean... Where would you stand?
And when she is condemned to an unimaginably painful death?.. Where would you then stand? Beside her?

Warrior Girl is a heart-stopping retelling of the legend of St. Joan of Arc. Written from the point of view of Joan's cousin, Mariane De Courcey, the story convinces the reader that men aren't the only brave soldiers out there. Their combined story becomes one of betrayal, bravery, passion and battle.

'The healing revelation with which this novel ends is so unexpected and utterly right that it made me gulp.' Kevin Crossley-Holland, (The Guardian)

'The Jewellers Skin' by Ruth Valentine ISBN: 978-0-9548373-4-1

1946… England is recovering from war and change is upon everything. Nadia Humphreys is resident Cook at Holywell, a Victorian asylum on the outskirts of London, but now her past is coming to light, threatening not only her livelihood but also her hard-won sanity. Reaching from Kosovo to London and told with great insight and humour in vivid, luminous prose, The Jewellers Skin is an incredibly powerful Debut Novel from Ruth Valentine.

'The Ophelia Box' by Jenny Rodwell ISBN: 978-0-9930424-1-6

Beautifully crafted, this Debut Novel by Derbyshire based author Jenny Rodwell intrigues from the first lines. Her wonderfully dysfunctional characters are immediately recognisable and painted with such clarity that by the end of the first chapter we begin to wonder if we are not all somehow related…

Entered by Cybermouse Books for The Costa First Novel Awards 2015

'The Ophelia Box is written with an ingenious wit that made me smile long after I closed the lid…'
Bryony Doran, (Author of 'The China Bird' and 'The Sand Eggs')

'11 o'clock Chocolate Cake' by Caroline Pitcher
ISBN: 978-0-9548373-5-8

This book is an important part of the library of ANY pre-teen/early teen girl. Discover the joys and anxieties of turning sixteen even before you get there! Find the location of 'The Most Important Bus Stop At The Very Centre Of The Universe!' (*And make all of the six wonderful recipes in the book along the way…*)

'This is the story of a Summer just gone. It's the story of Lizzie and Star and Me, of Dodo, Pram Gran, Bottom Bob and Boss Woman, Tuba Boy… and the Beautiful Stranger… Who's telling this story? ME! Emma Peek. Life changed for us all this Summer.'

'A Day for Tigers' by Bill Allerton ASIN: B00IN3Q9PQ

A Slipstream Science Fiction Novella for E-Readers [Kindle Edition]

Written in vividly lyrical prose and set against the backdrop of a three Cosmonaut mission to explore the asteroid belt, *A Day For Tigers* becomes an unflinching exploration of inner spaces, where each part is as vital to survival as the other, until the inevitable conflict between revealed emotion and unbridled ego shifts the balance into chaos.

Included at the end of the novella are full characterisations of the Cosmonauts, a word from the author, and the entire original poem from which the story was derived.

'Watch & Wait… *A Timeless Anthology'* ISBN: 978-0-9548373-1-0

A collection of superb short works dedicated to 'Andrew', and all others living with Lymphoma.

Twenty authors… household names or major prize winners alongside others who soon will be… have gifted their short stories freely to this outstanding collection. The stories are eclectic, strangely familiar, or great and good fun. They will question your perception and challenge your accepted view of life and literature.

ALL proceeds from the sale of this anthology are gifted by the publisher directly to The Lymphoma Association (Registered Charity no. 1068395) http://www.lymphomas.org.uk

'Requiem' by Berlie Doherty   ISBN: 978-0-9548373-9-6

Set in both Ireland and Venice, Requiem follows the life and career of Opera star Cecelia Deardon. Probing the tragi-comedy of an Irish convent upbringing with a rare power and sensitivity, Requiem continues to disturb the reader long after the book is finished.

'I have great feelings of admiration for Requiem. This is a very good book indeed' Beryl Bainbridge

'Mine' by Caroline Pitcher ISBN: 978-0-9548373-8-9

Left alone in the Derbyshire cottage she has moved into with her mother, step-father and annoying brother, Shelley hears ancient and troubled voices, echoes from another time held within the thick stone walls for hundreds of years and now reaching out to her... Can Shelley help them find peace and, through that, can they help her to find her *own* identity? '*It's not MINE...*' she says, '*Nothing is...*'

Written for the early teenage 'outsider', 'Mine' places the search for identity into several historical contexts, showing how only *some* things change through time.

'*Vivid, beautifully written, I couldn't put it down...*' Nicola Ho

Our books are available from all good bookshops, from Amazon and Amazon for Kindle, or direct from ourselves at; http://www.cybermouse-multimedia.com